Fuzzy Baseball

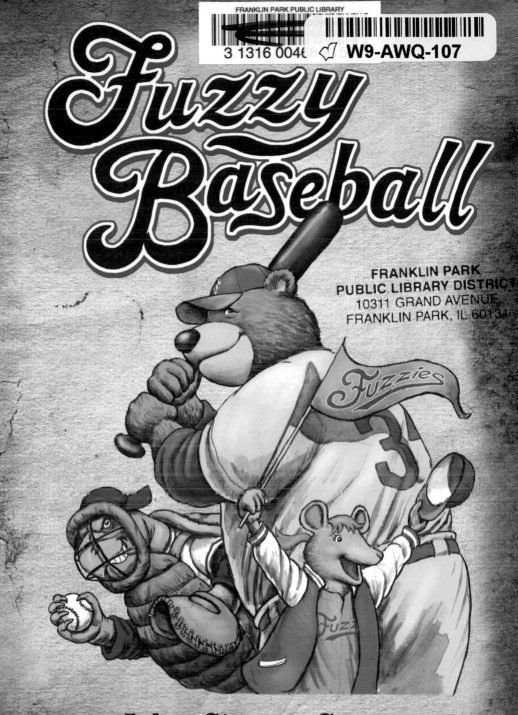

John Steven Gurney

PAPERCUTZ™
New York

Fuzzy Baseball

Created by John Steven Gurney

Dawn Guzzo – Design and Production

Jeff Whitman – Production Coordinator

Shannon Eric Denton – Editor

Bethany Bryan – Associate Editor

Jim Salicrup
Editor-in-Chief

Fuzzy Baseball Copyright © 2016 by John Steven Gurney
All other editorial material © 2016 by Papercutz

ISBN PB: 978-1-62991-477-0
ISBN HC: 978-1-5458-0435-3

Printed in India

Papercutz books may be purchased for business or promotional use.
For information on bulk purchases please contact
Macmillan Corporate and Premium Sales Department at
(800) 221-7945 x5442.

Distributed by Macmillan
2nd printing, March 2019

JOHN STEVEN GURNEY

Fuzzy Baseball

For Molly, Jesse, Kathie,
and three World Champion teams:
The 1980 Philadelphia Phillies,
The 1986 New York Mets,
and The 2004 Boston Red Sox

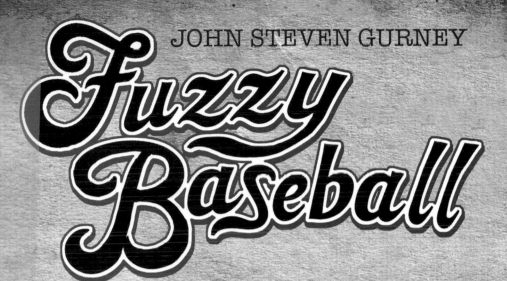

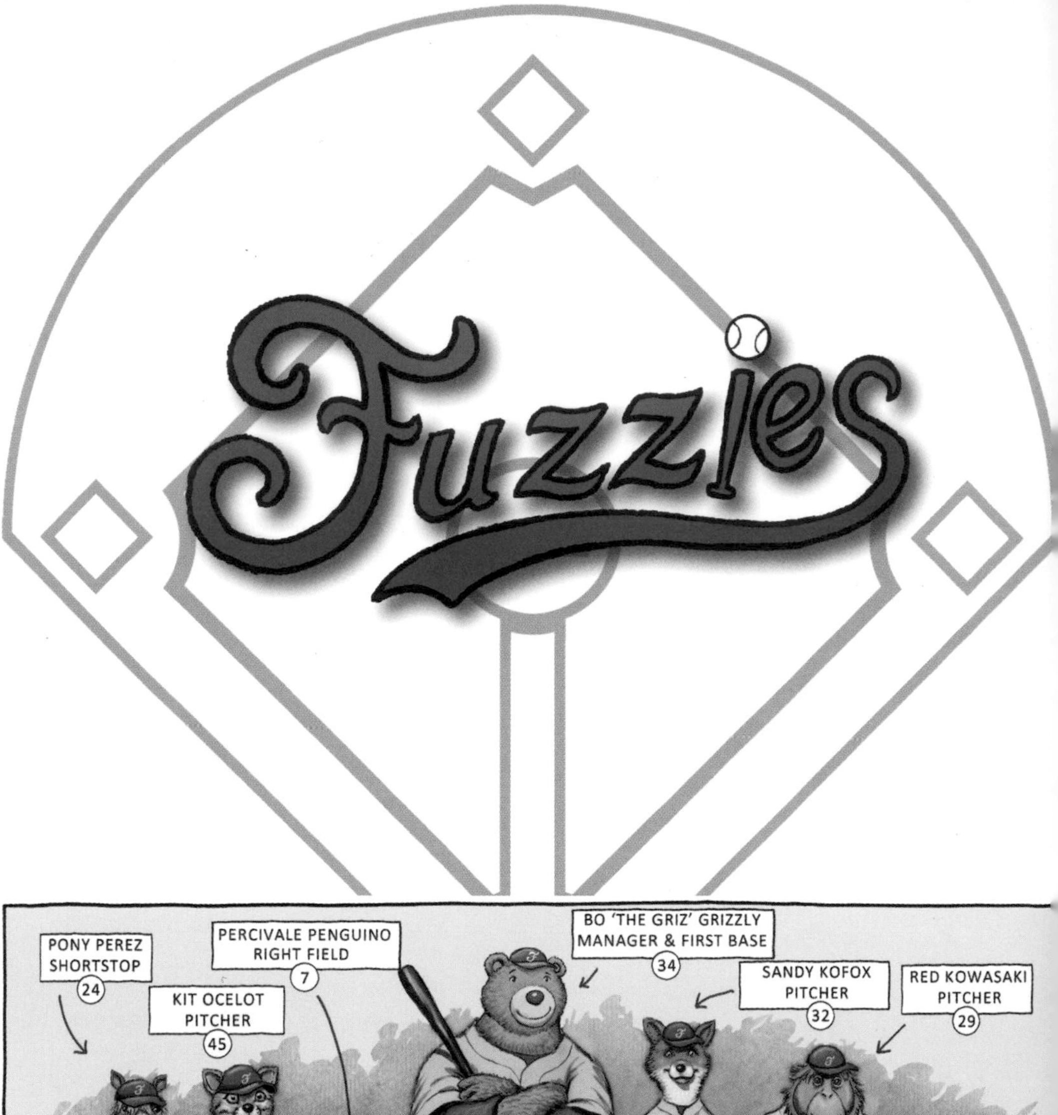

Fuzzies

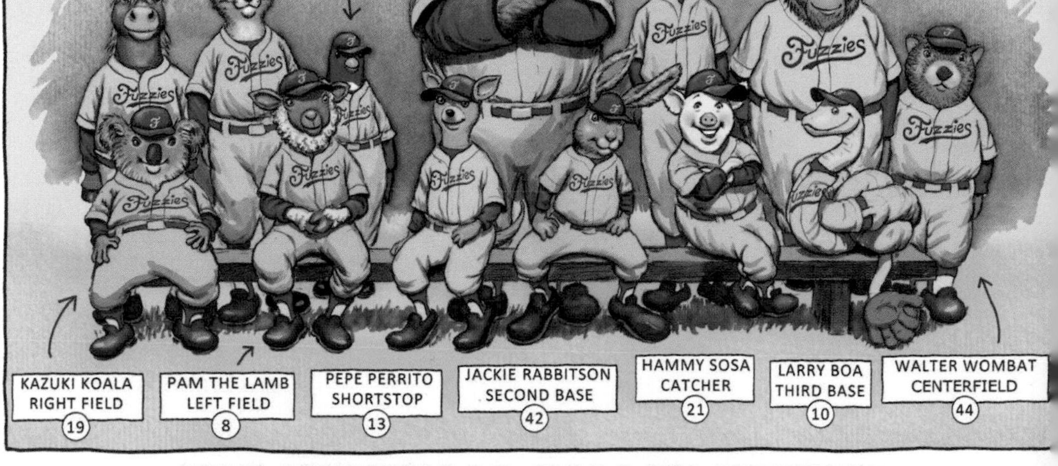

PONY PEREZ SHORTSTOP 24
PERCIVALE PENGUINO RIGHT FIELD 7
KIT OCELOT PITCHER 45
BO 'THE GRIZ' GRIZZLY MANAGER & FIRST BASE 34
SANDY KOFOX PITCHER 32
RED KOWASAKI PITCHER 29
KAZUKI KOALA RIGHT FIELD 19
PAM THE LAMB LEFT FIELD 8
PEPE PERRITO SHORTSTOP 13
JACKIE RABBITSON SECOND BASE 42
HAMMY SOSA CATCHER 21
LARRY BOA THIRD BASE 10
WALTER WOMBAT CENTERFIELD 44

THE FERNWOOD VALLEY FUZZIES

RED CLAWS

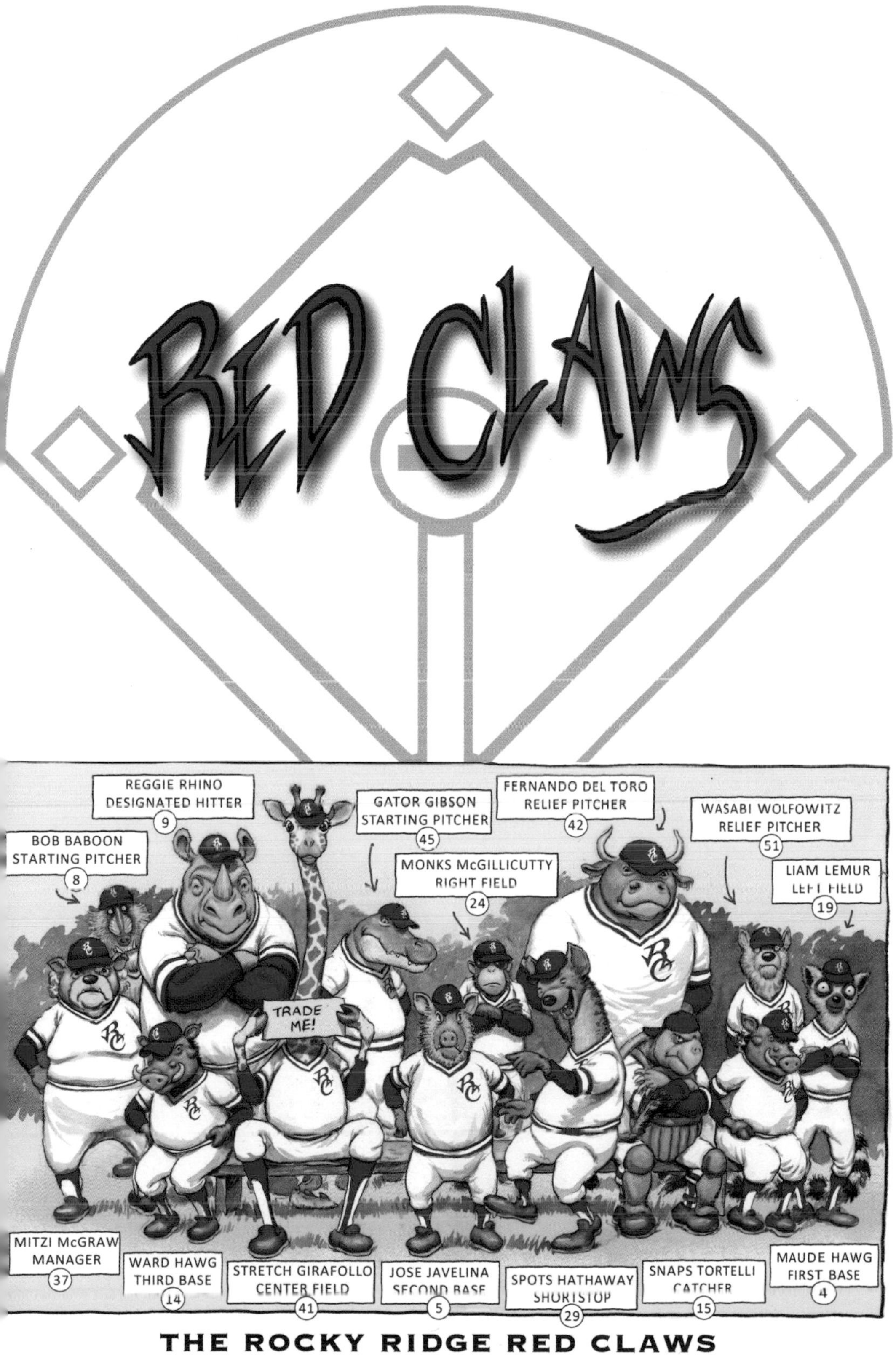

REGGIE RHINO DESIGNATED HITTER 9
GATOR GIBSON STARTING PITCHER 45
FERNANDO DEL TORO RELIEF PITCHER 42
WASABI WOLFOWITZ RELIEF PITCHER 51
BOB BABOON STARTING PITCHER 8
MONKS McGILLICUTTY RIGHT FIELD 24
LIAM LEMUR LEFT FIELD 19
TRADE ME!
MITZI McGRAW MANAGER 37
WARD HAWG THIRD BASE 14
STRETCH GIRAFOLLO CENTER FIELD 41
JOSE JAVELINA SECOND BASE 5
SPOTS HATHAWAY SHORTSTOP 29
SNAPS TORTELLI CATCHER 15
MAUDE HAWG FIRST BASE 4

THE ROCKY RIDGE RED CLAWS

INTRODUCING THE FERNWOOD VALLEY

Fuzzies

THESE ARE THE GOOD GUYS!

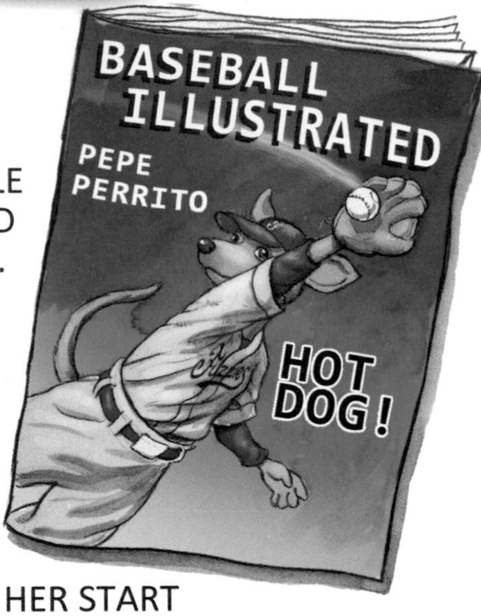
BASEBALL ILLUSTRATED
PEPE PERRITO
HOT DOG!

THIS LITTLE DOG HAS SPEED AND SMARTS.

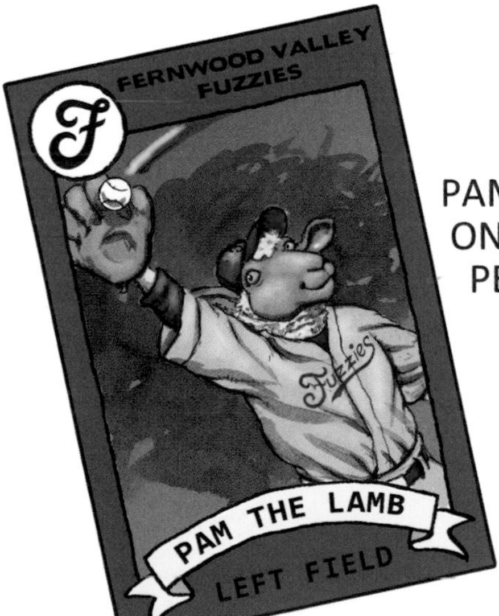
FERNWOOD VALLEY FUZZIES
F
Fuzzies
PAM THE LAMB
LEFT FIELD

PAM GOT HER START ON THE FUZZIES' PETTING FARM TEAM.

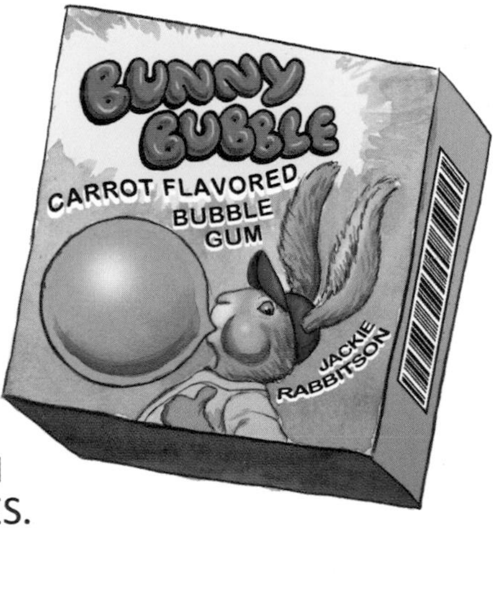
BUNNY BUBBLE
CARROT FLAVORED BUBBLE GUM
JACKIE RABBITSON

JACKIE RABBITSON- FASTEST FEET IN THE BIG LEAGUES.

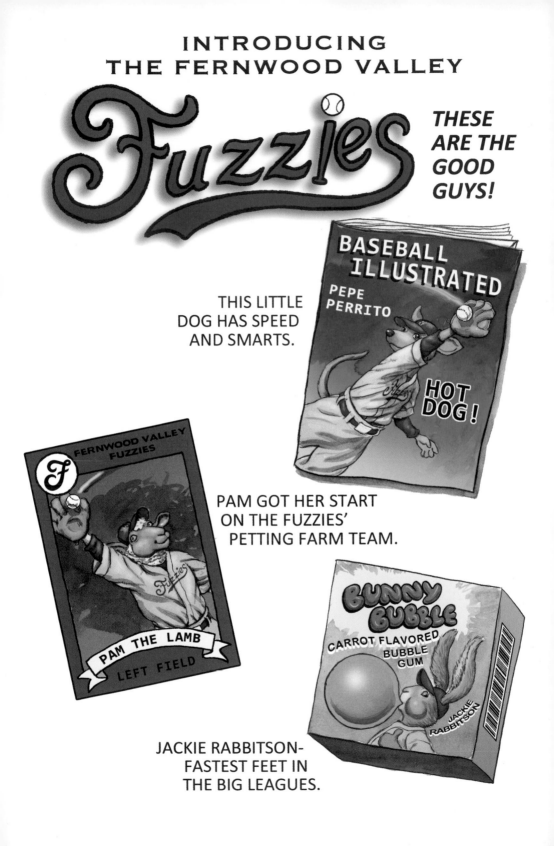

BO “THE GRIZ” GRIZZLY-
ALL STAR SLUGGER
AND MANAGER.

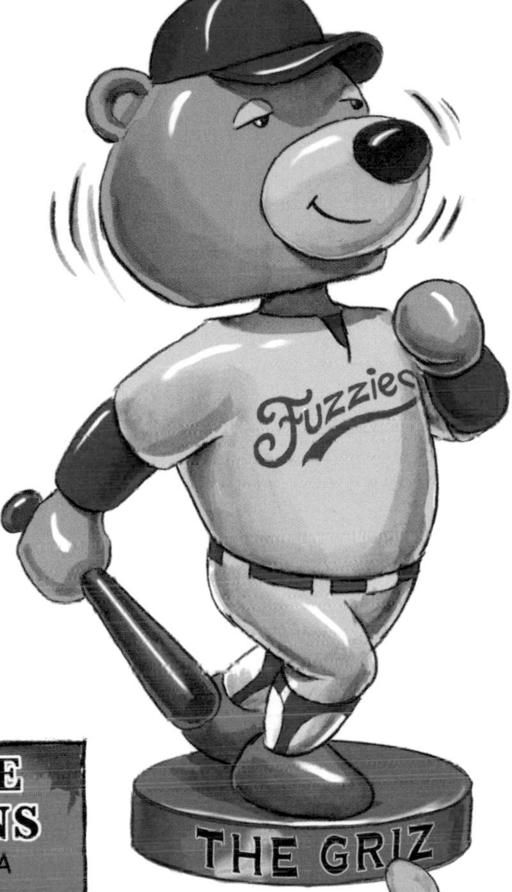
Fuzzies
THE GRIZ

HAMMY SOSA - THE FUZZIES’
CONFIDENT CATCHER

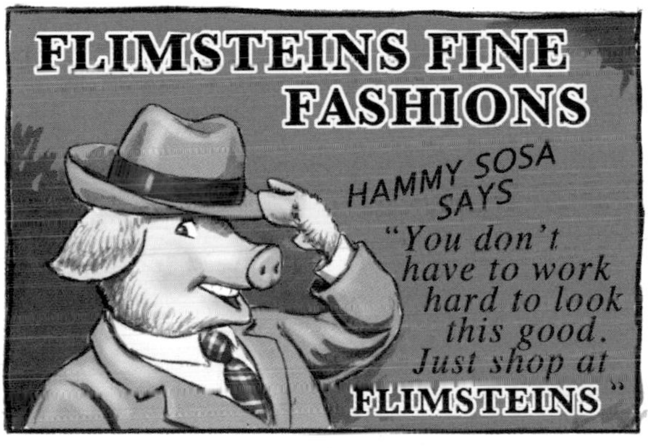
FLIMSTEINS FINE FASHIONS
HAMMY SOSA SAYS
“You don’t have to work hard to look this good. Just shop at FLIMSTEINS”

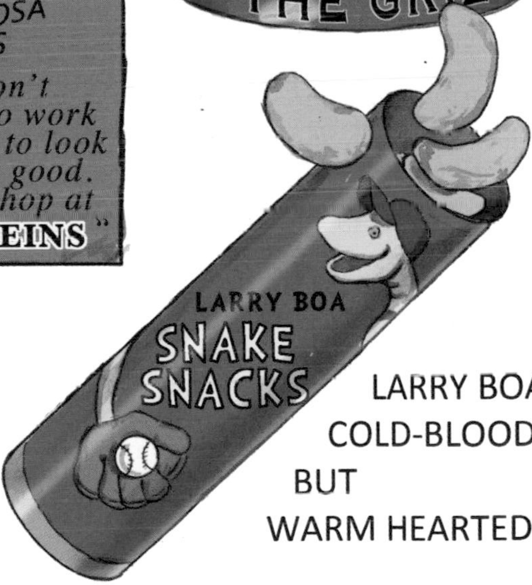
LARRY BOA
SNAKE SNACKS

LARRY BOA-
COLD-BLOODED,
BUT
WARM HEARTED

YET, DESPITE ALL THIS TALENT, THE FUZZIES ALWAYS LOST TO THE ROCKY RIDGE RED CLAWS.

INTRODUCING

THE ROCKY RIDGE RED CLAWS

THESE ARE THE BAD GUYS!

THE THREE MAIN REASONS
THAT THE FUZZIES
CAN'T SCORE AGAINST
THE RED CLAWS

FIELDING

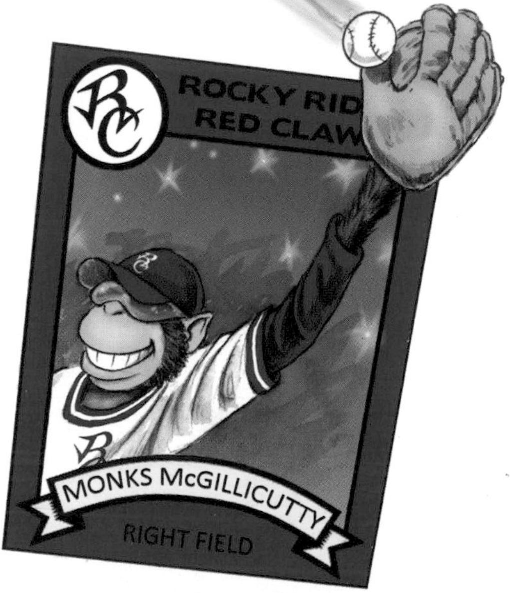
ROCKY RIDGE RED CLAWS
MONKS McGILLICUTTY
RIGHT FIELD

PITCHING

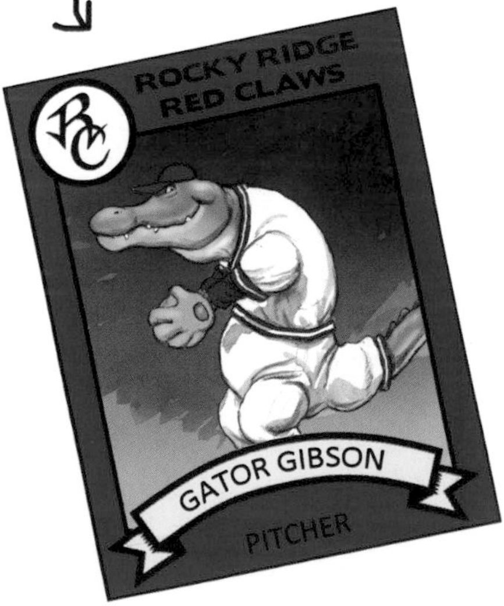
ROCKY RIDGE RED CLAWS
GATOR GIBSON
PITCHER

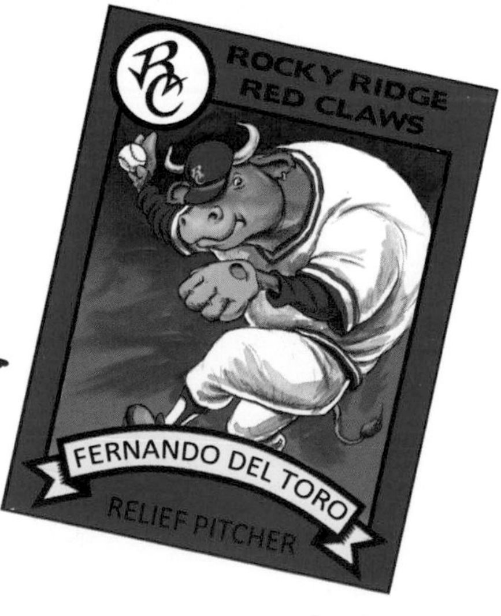
ROCKY RIDGE RED CLAWS
FERNANDO DEL TORO
RELIEF PITCHER

MORE PITCHING

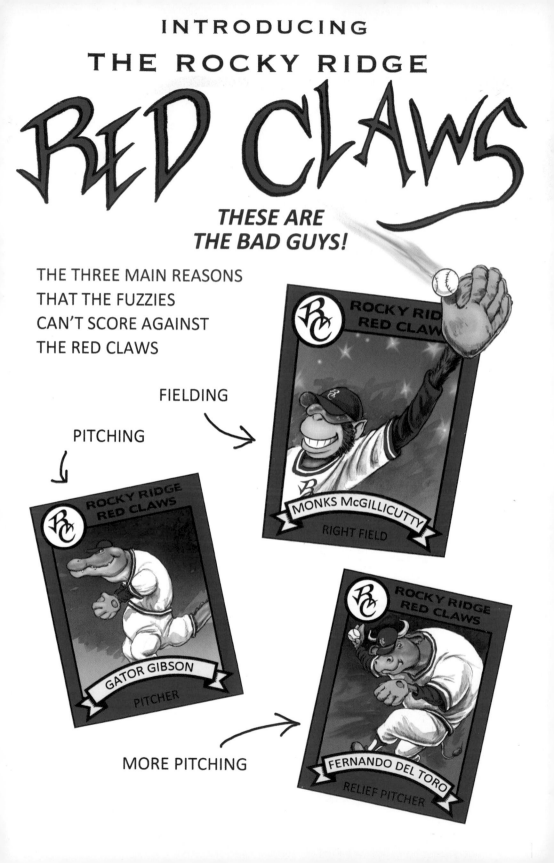

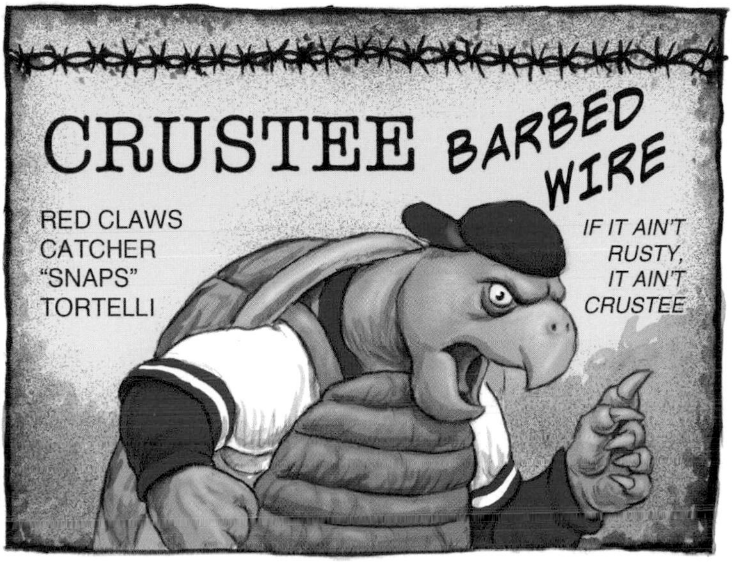
CRUSTEE
BARBED WIRE
RED CLAWS CATCHER "SNAPS" TORTELLI
IF IT AIN'T RUSTY, IT AIN'T CRUSTEE

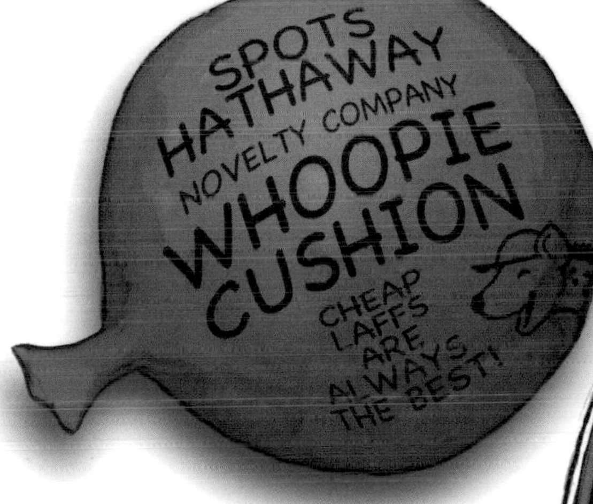
SPOTS HATHAWAY
NOVELTY COMPANY
WHOOPIE CUSHION
CHEAP LAFFS ARE ALWAYS THE BEST!

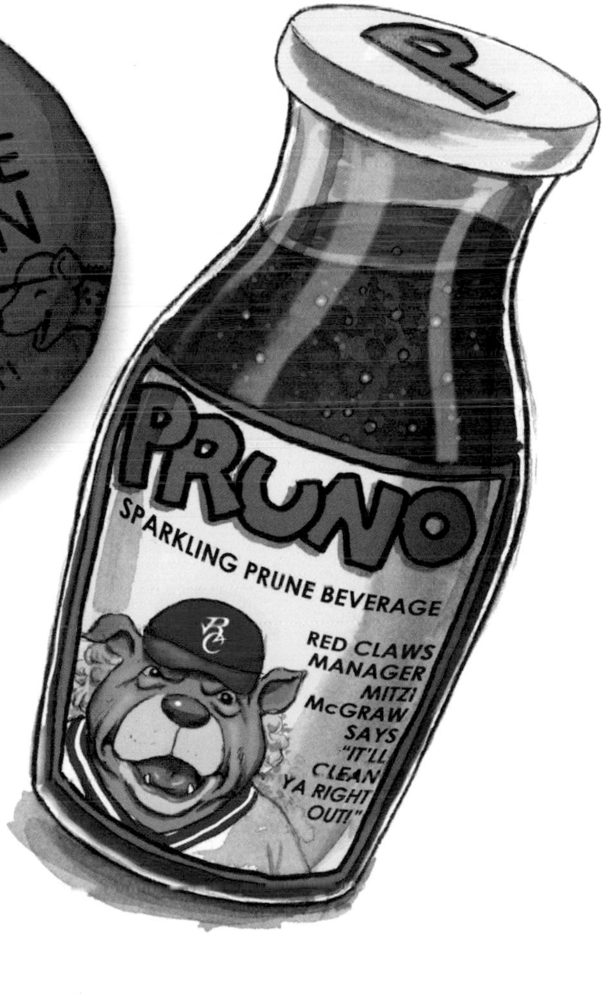
P
PRUNO
SPARKLING PRUNE BEVERAGE
RC
RED CLAWS MANAGER MITZI McGRAW SAYS "IT'LL CLEAN YA RIGHT OUT!"

WAS THERE ANYONE OUT THERE WHO BELIEVED THAT THE FUZZIES COULD BEAT THE RED CLAWS?

INTRODUCING

BLOSSOM HONEY POSSUM

THE WORLD'S BIGGEST FERNWOOD VALLEY FUZZIES FAN

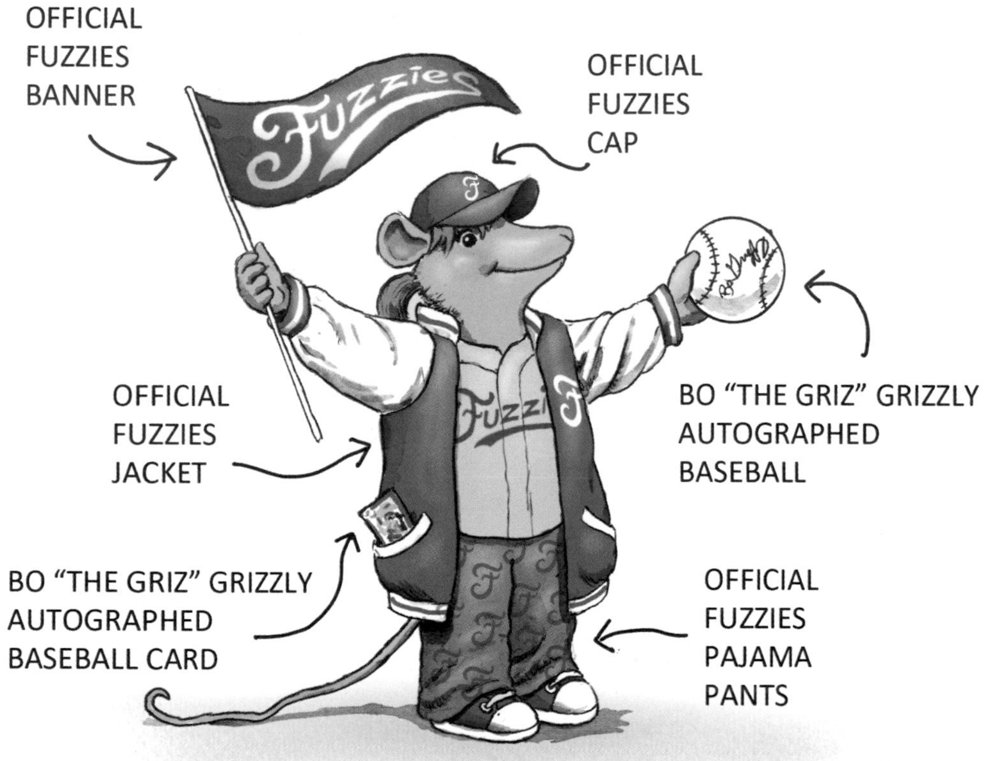

OFFICIAL FUZZIES BANNER
OFFICIAL FUZZIES CAP
Fuzzies
OFFICIAL FUZZIES JACKET
BO "THE GRIZ" GRIZZLY AUTOGRAPHED BASEBALL
BO "THE GRIZ" GRIZZLY AUTOGRAPHED BASEBALL CARD
OFFICIAL FUZZIES PAJAMA PANTS

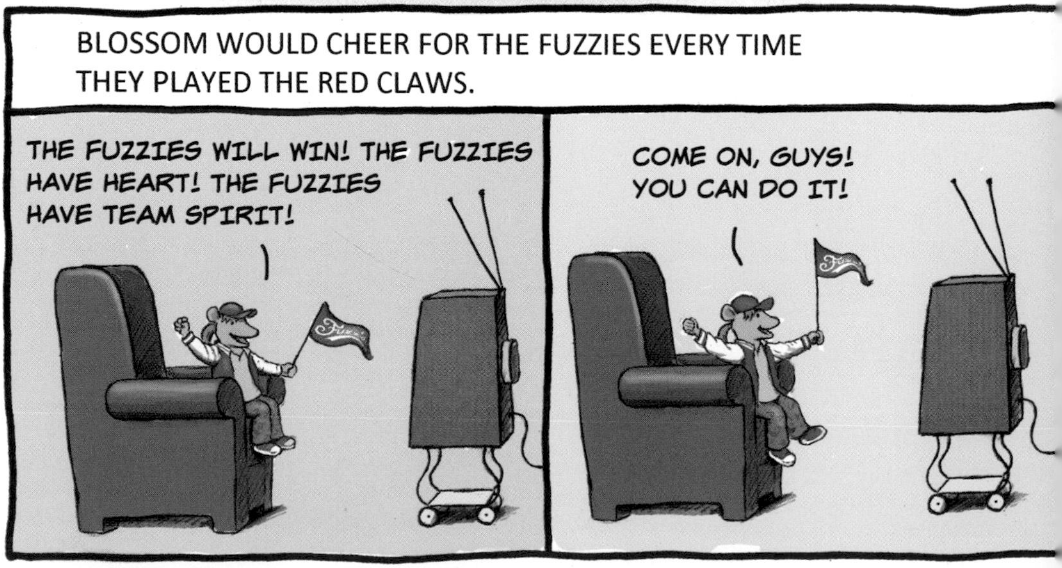

BLOSSOM WOULD CHEER FOR THE FUZZIES EVERY TIME THEY PLAYED THE RED CLAWS.
THE FUZZIES WILL WIN! THE FUZZIES HAVE HEART! THE FUZZIES HAVE TEAM SPIRIT!
COME ON, GUYS! YOU CAN DO IT!

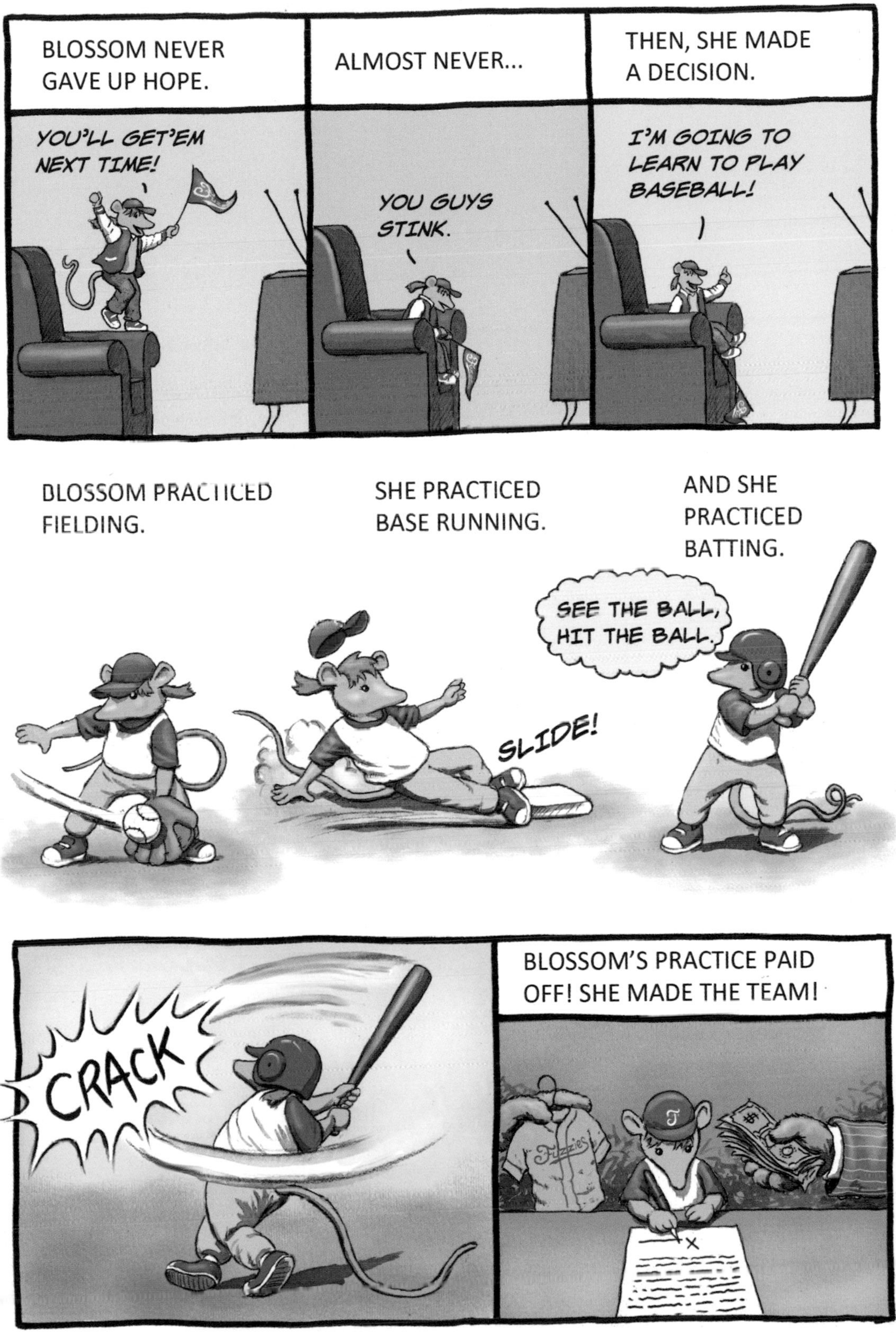
BLOSSOM NEVER GAVE UP HOPE.
YOU'LL GET'EM NEXT TIME!
ALMOST NEVER...
YOU GUYS STINK.
THEN, SHE MADE A DECISION.
I'M GOING TO LEARN TO PLAY BASEBALL!
BLOSSOM PRACTICED FIELDING.
SHE PRACTICED BASE RUNNING.
SLIDE!
AND SHE PRACTICED BATTING.
SEE THE BALL, HIT THE BALL.
CRACK
BLOSSOM'S PRACTICE PAID OFF! SHE MADE THE TEAM!
Fuzzies

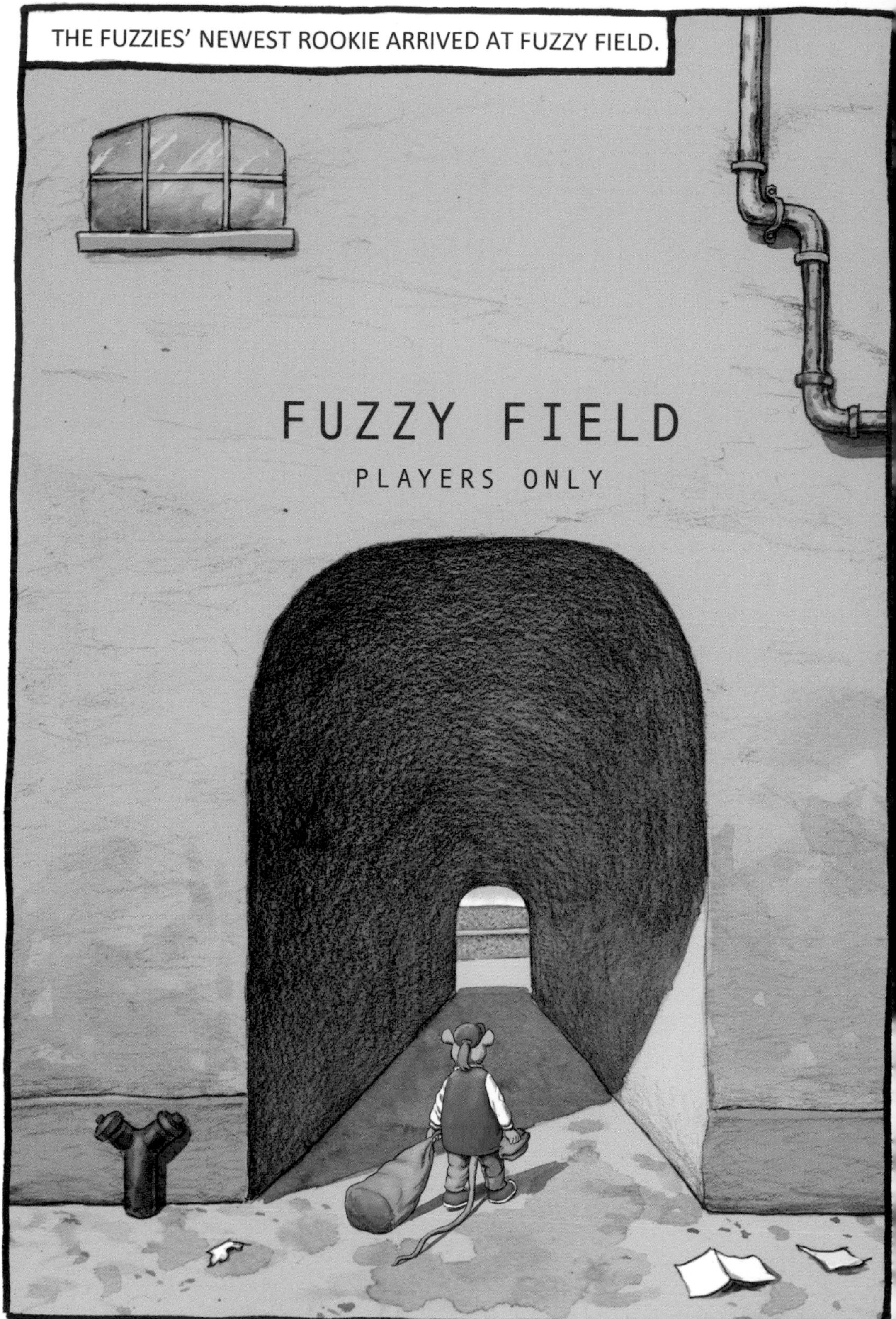
THE FUZZIES' NEWEST ROOKIE ARRIVED AT FUZZY FIELD.
FUZZY FIELD
PLAYERS ONLY

GAME DAY

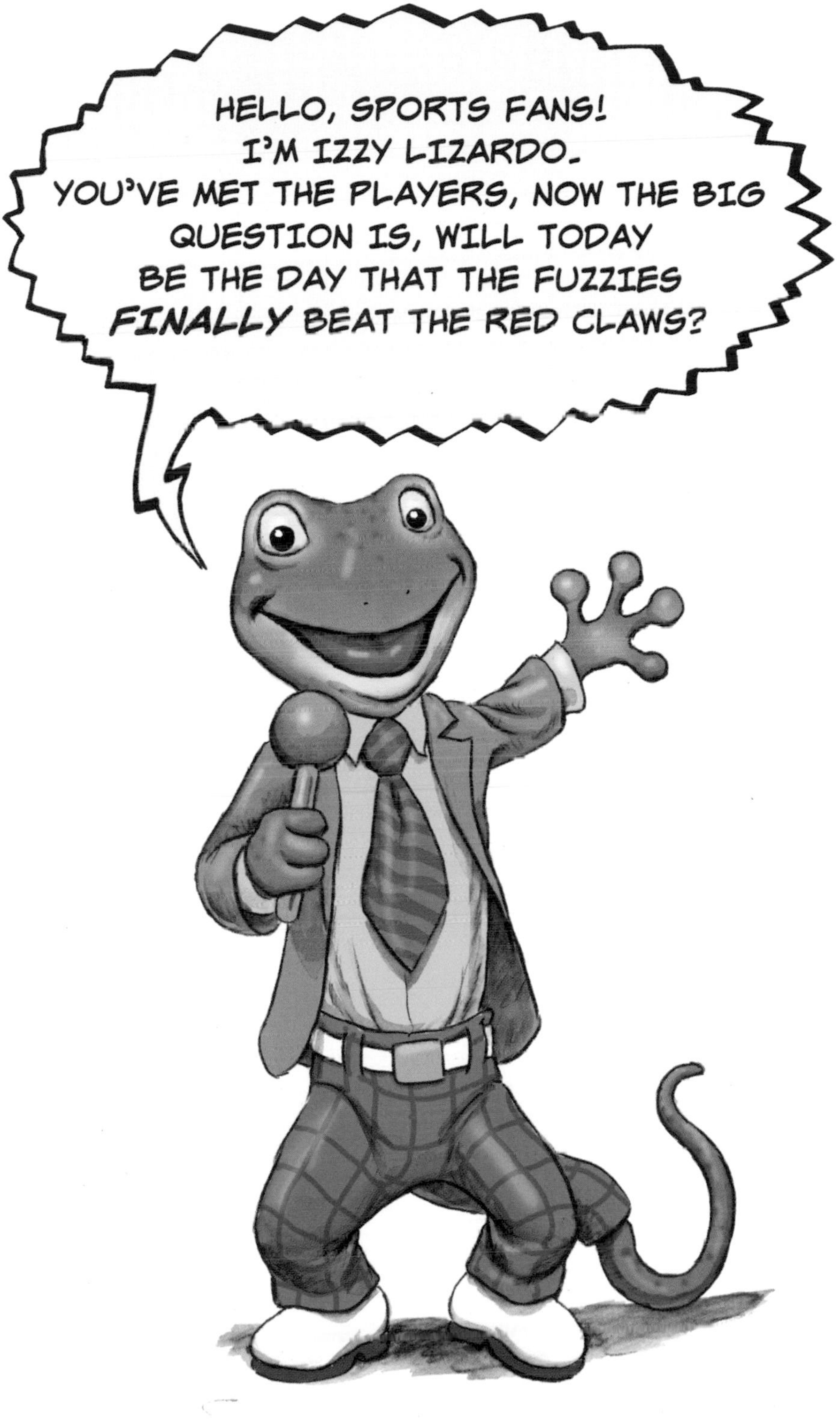
HELLO, SPORTS FANS!
I'M IZZY LIZARDO.
YOU'VE MET THE PLAYERS, NOW THE BIG QUESTION IS, WILL TODAY BE THE DAY THAT THE FUZZIES *FINALLY* BEAT THE RED CLAWS?

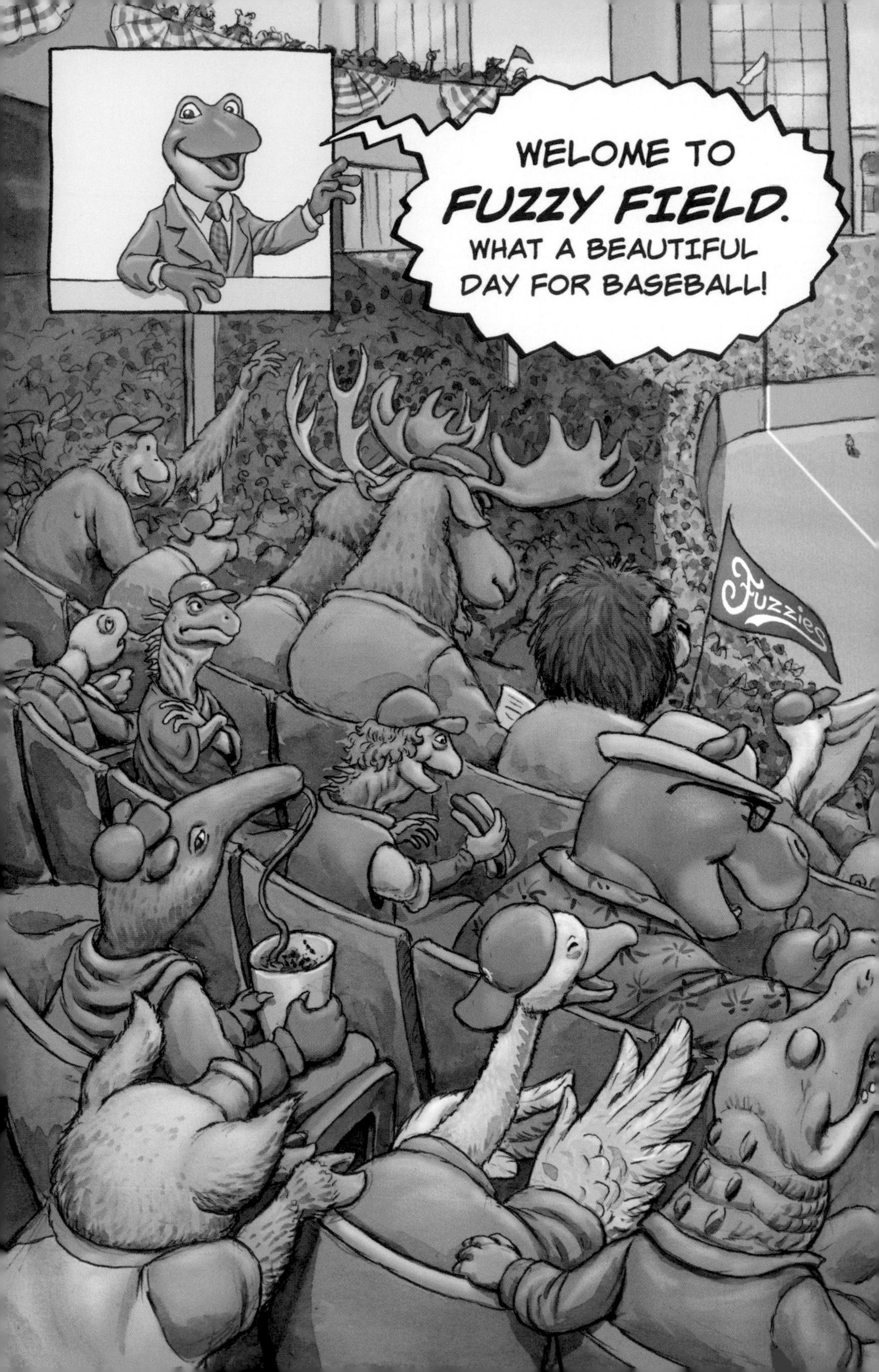
WELOME TO
FUZZY FIELD.
WHAT A BEAUTIFUL
DAY FOR BASEBALL!
Fuzzies

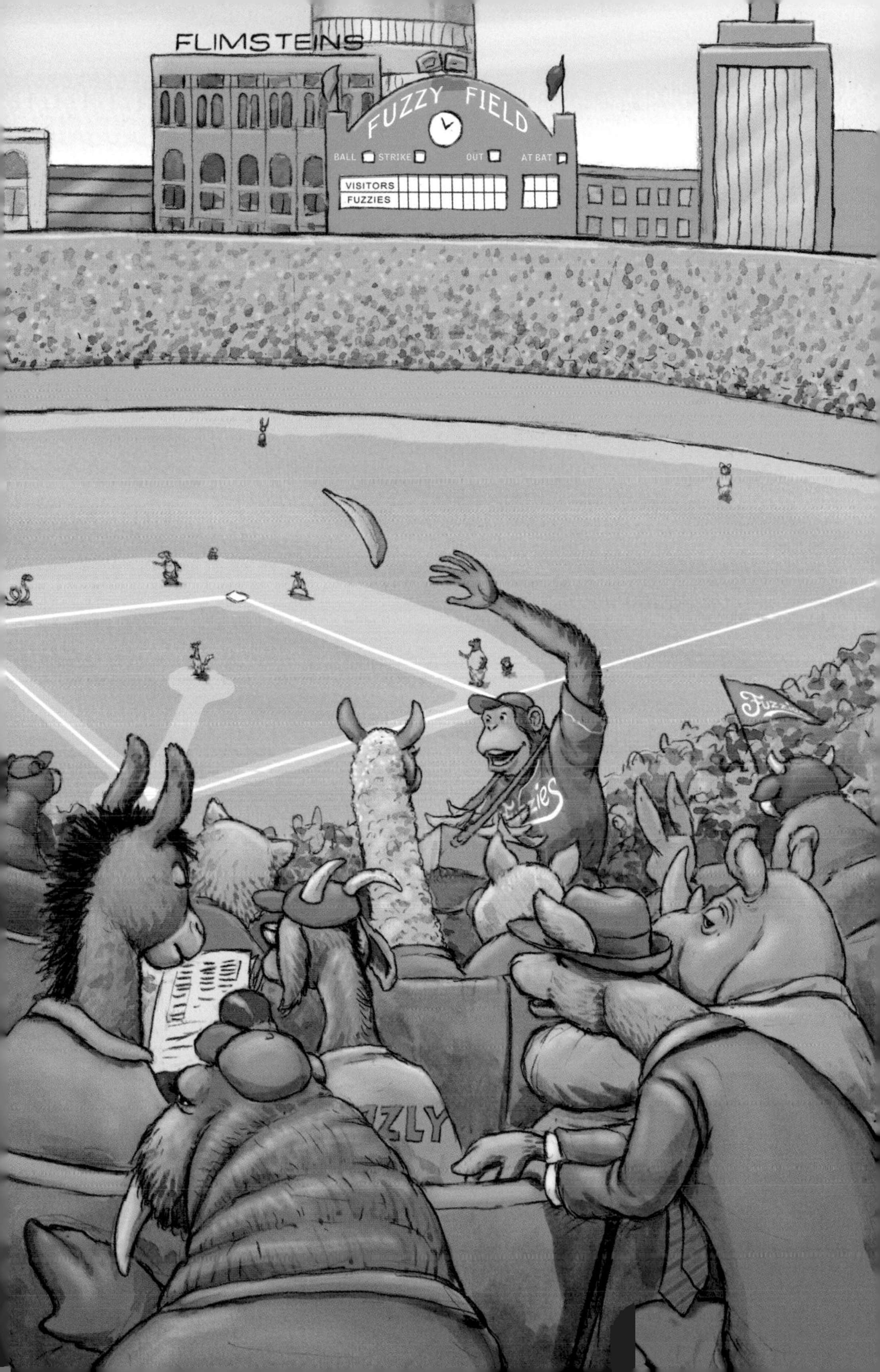
FLIMSTEINS
FUZZY FIELD
BALL
STRIKE
OUT
AT BAT
VISITORS
FUZZIES

THE FIRST EIGHT-AND-A-HALF INNINGS DID NOT GO WELL FOR THE FUZZIES.

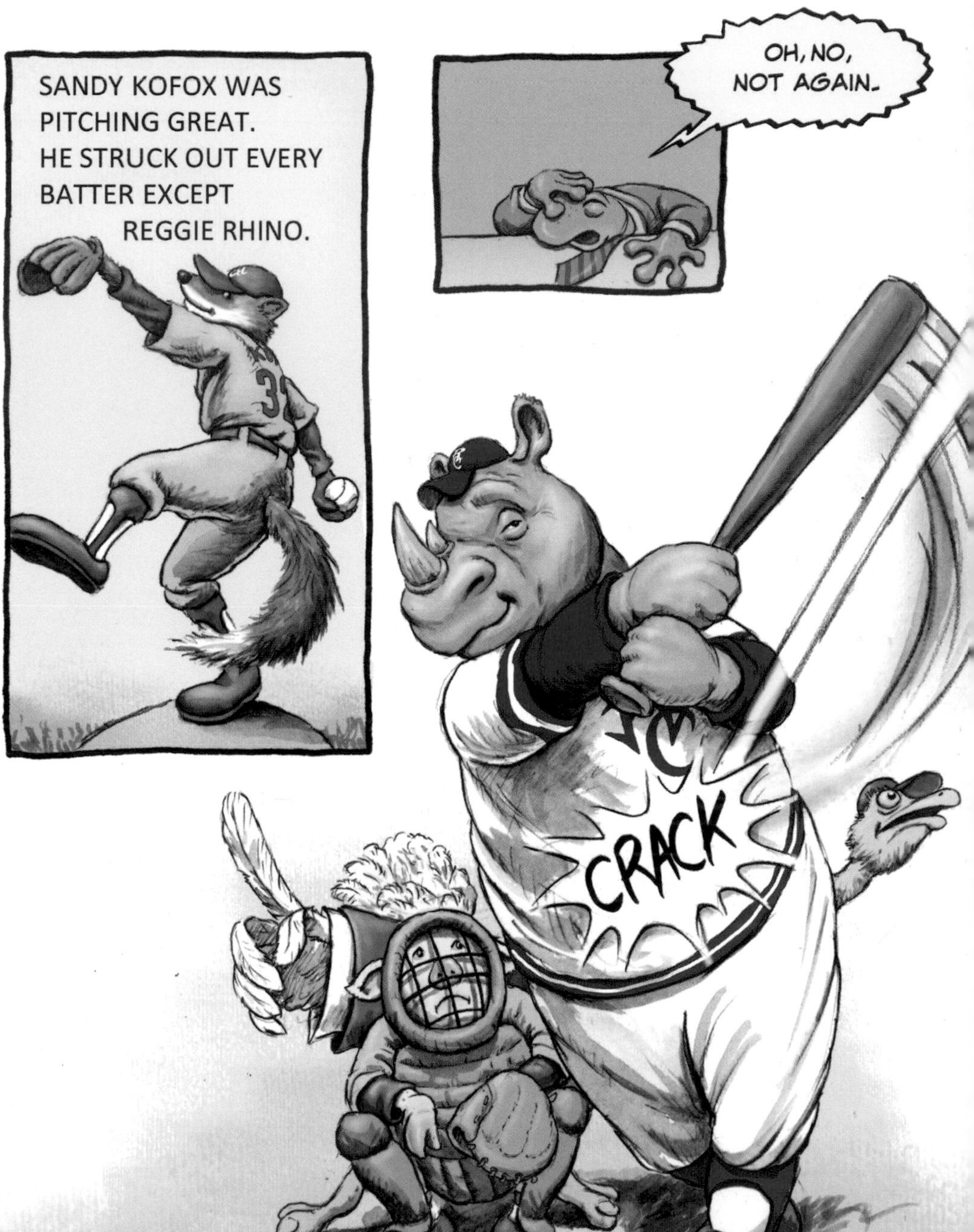
SANDY KOFOX WAS PITCHING GREAT. HE STRUCK OUT EVERY BATTER EXCEPT REGGIE RHINO.
OH, NO, NOT AGAIN.
CRACK

UNFORTUNATELY, EVERY TIME REGGIE RHINO WAS UP HE HIT A HOME RUN. AND HE WAS UP THREE TIMES.

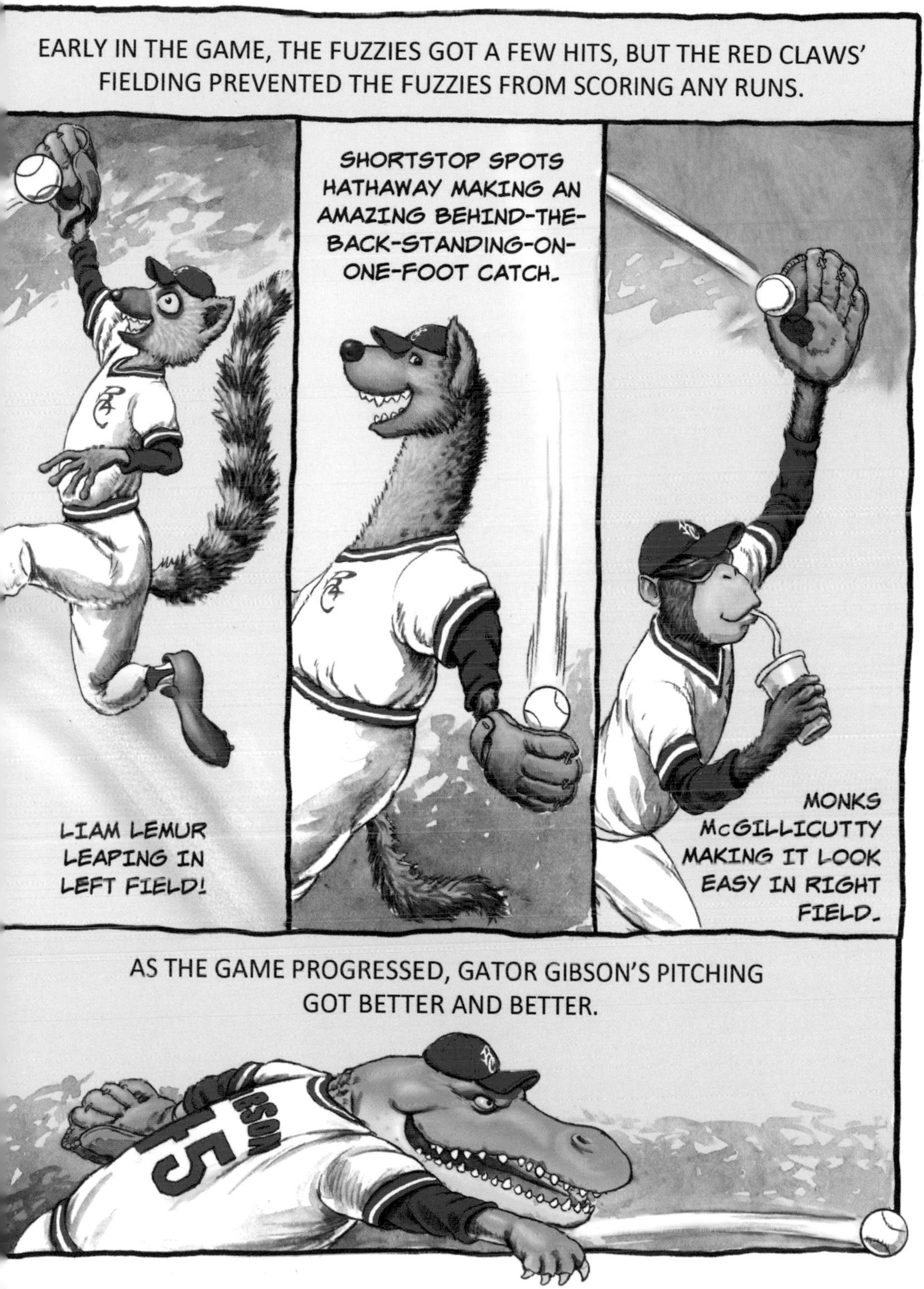
EARLY IN THE GAME, THE FUZZIES GOT A FEW HITS, BUT THE RED CLAWS' FIELDING PREVENTED THE FUZZIES FROM SCORING ANY RUNS.
LIAM LEMUR LEAPING IN LEFT FIELD!
SHORTSTOP SPOTS HATHAWAY MAKING AN AMAZING BEHIND-THE-BACK-STANDING-ON-ONE-FOOT CATCH.
MONKS McGILLICUTTY MAKING IT LOOK EASY IN RIGHT FIELD.
AS THE GAME PROGRESSED, GATOR GIBSON'S PITCHING GOT BETTER AND BETTER.
15

BY THE NINTH INNING HIS PITCHES WERE UNHITTABLE.

THE BOTTOM OF THE NINTH INNING. THE FUZZIES' LAST CHANCE.

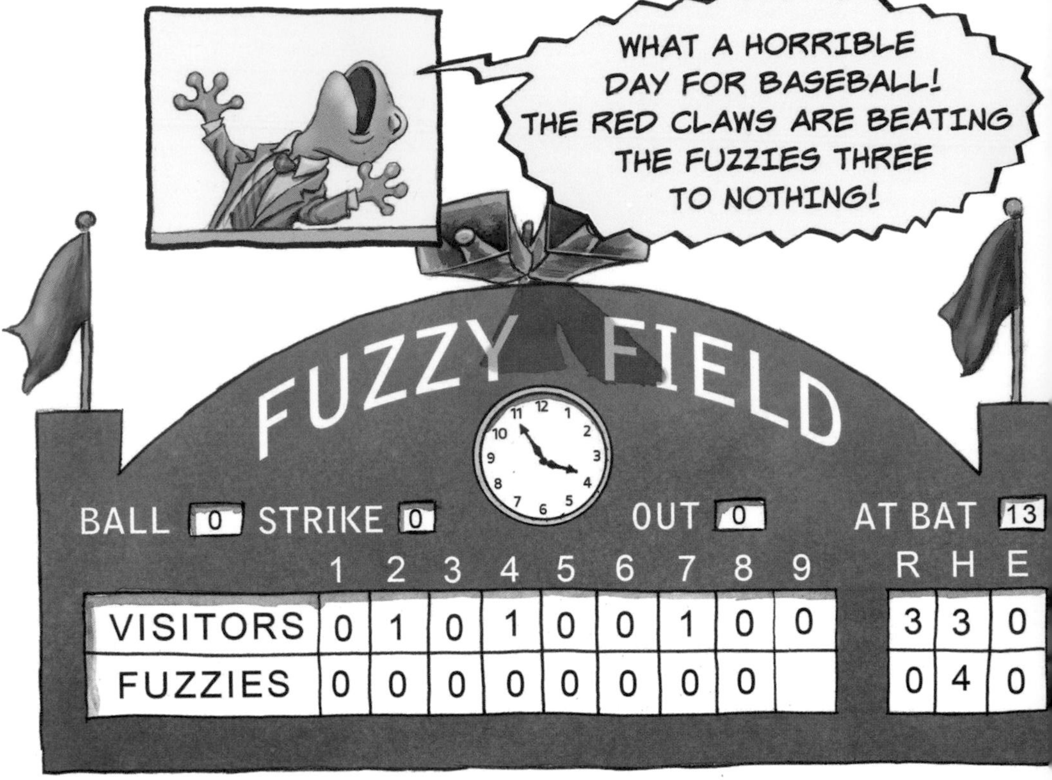
WHAT A HORRIBLE DAY FOR BASEBALL! THE RED CLAWS ARE BEATING THE FUZZIES THREE TO NOTHING!
FUZZY FIELD
BALL 0 STRIKE 0 OUT 0 AT BAT 13
1 2 3 4 5 6 7 8 9 R H E
VISITORS 0 1 0 1 0 0 1 0 0 3 3 0
FUZZIES 0 0 0 0 0 0 0 0 0 4 0

BLOSSOM WAS NOT SURPRISED THAT THE FUZZIES WERE LOSING. BUT SHE WAS SHOCKED AT HOW THEY WERE ACTING. THE FUZZIES DID NOT HAVE TEAM SPIRIT. THEY DID NOT HAVE HEART.

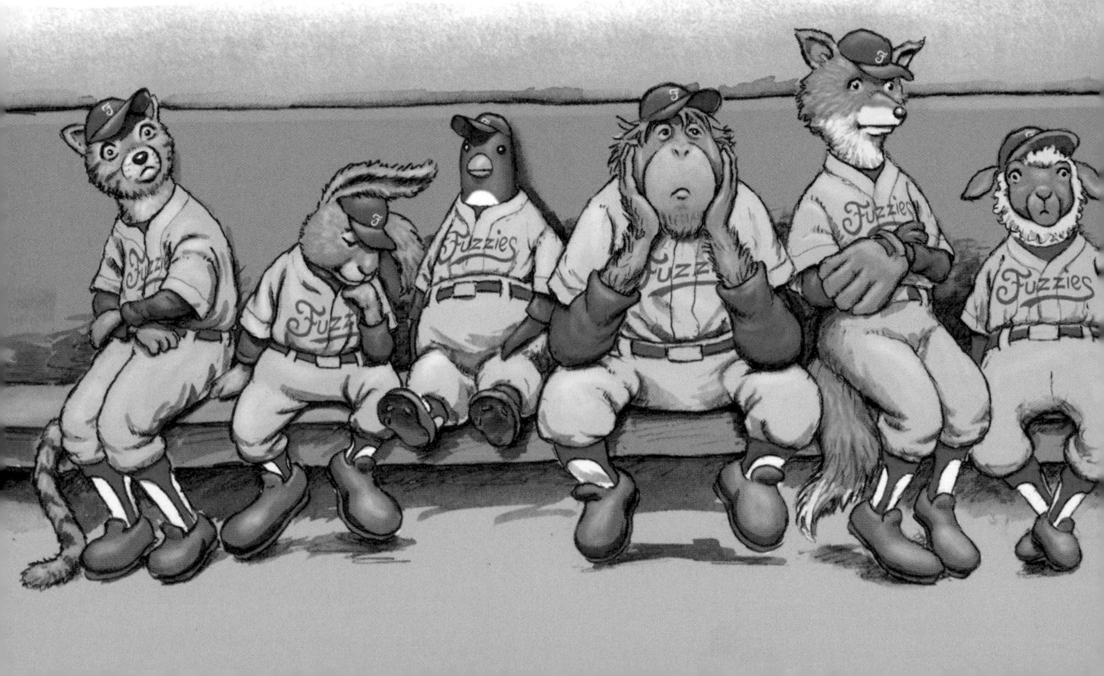
Fuzzies
Fuzzies
Fuzzies

THE RED CLAWS WERE SLAPPING THEIR PAWS AND SMACKING THEIR TAILS. THEY WERE HOOTING AND HOWLING AND GRUNTING AND MAKING FUN OF THE FUZZIES. THEY WERE ACTING LIKE A BUNCH OF... ANIMALS!

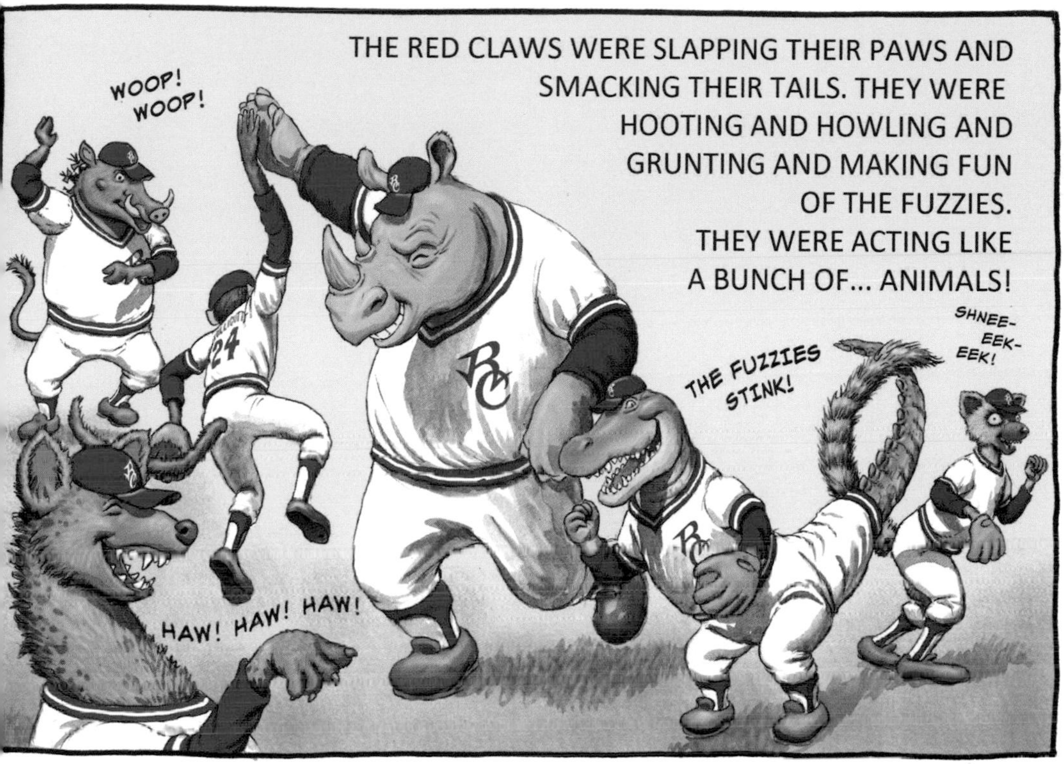
WOOP! WOOP!
24
RC
THE FUZZIES STINK!
SHNEE-EEK-EEK!
HAW! HAW! HAW!

THE WORST PART WAS THAT THE FUZZIES WERE ACTING LIKE A BUNCH OF LOSERS.

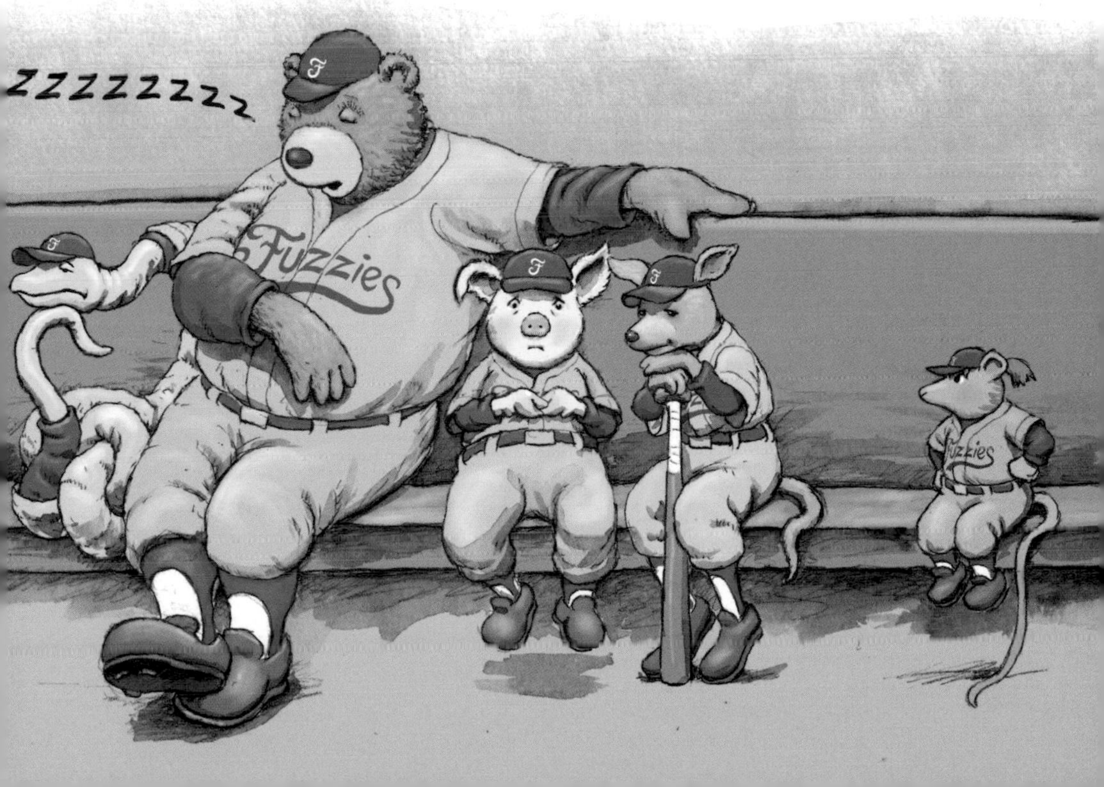
ZZZZZZZZZ
Fuzzies

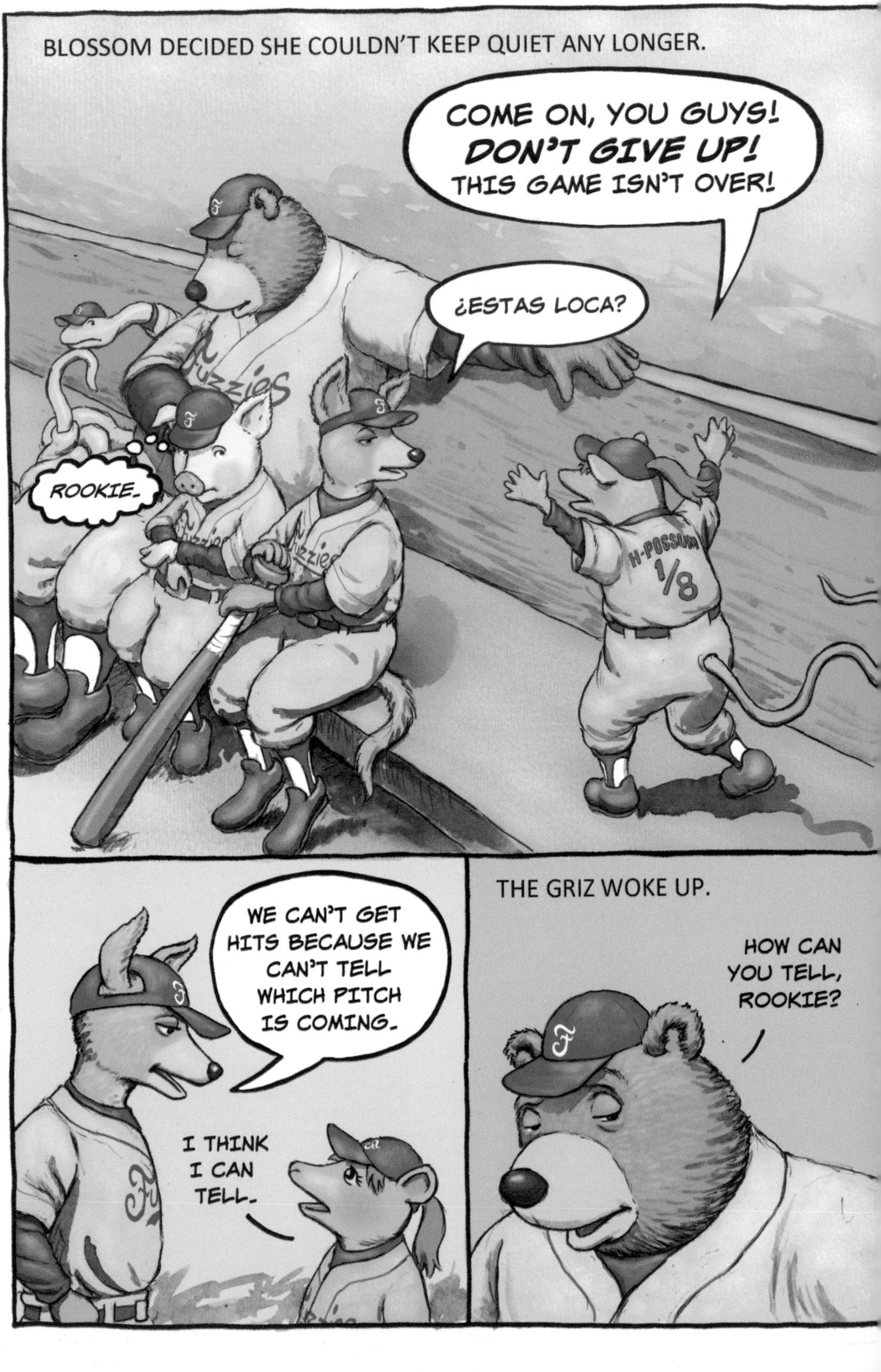
BLOSSOM DECIDED SHE COULDN'T KEEP QUIET ANY LONGER.
COME ON, YOU GUYS! DON'T GIVE UP! THIS GAME ISN'T OVER!
¿ESTAS LOCA?
ROOKIE.
H-POSSUM
1/8
WE CAN'T GET HITS BECAUSE WE CAN'T TELL WHICH PITCH IS COMING.
I THINK I CAN TELL.
THE GRIZ WOKE UP.
HOW CAN YOU TELL, ROOKIE?

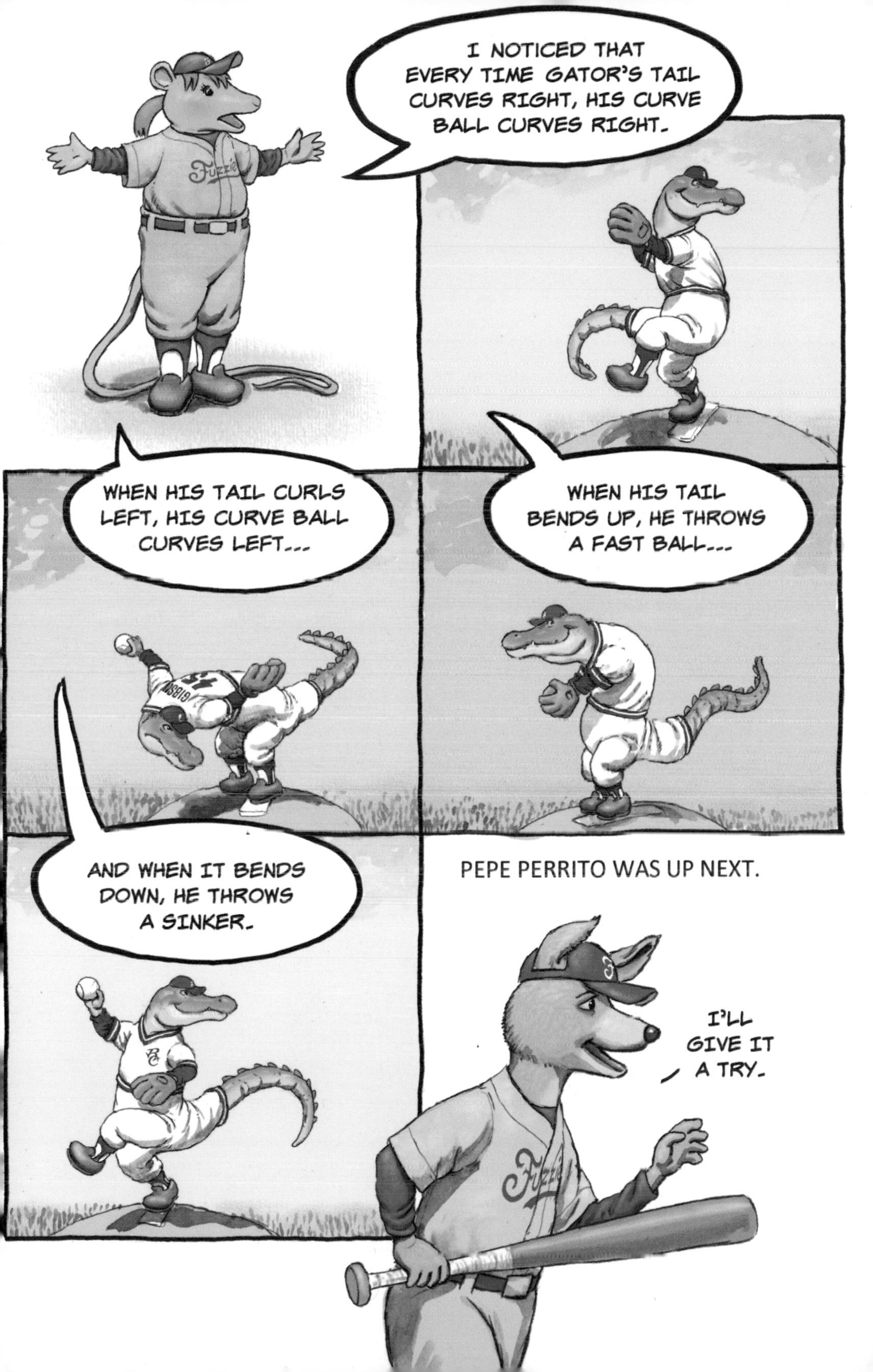
I NOTICED THAT EVERY TIME GATOR'S TAIL CURVES RIGHT, HIS CURVE BALL CURVES RIGHT.
WHEN HIS TAIL CURLS LEFT, HIS CURVE BALL CURVES LEFT...
WHEN HIS TAIL BENDS UP, HE THROWS A FAST BALL...
AND WHEN IT BENDS DOWN, HE THROWS A SINKER.
PEPE PERRITO WAS UP NEXT.
I'LL GIVE IT A TRY.

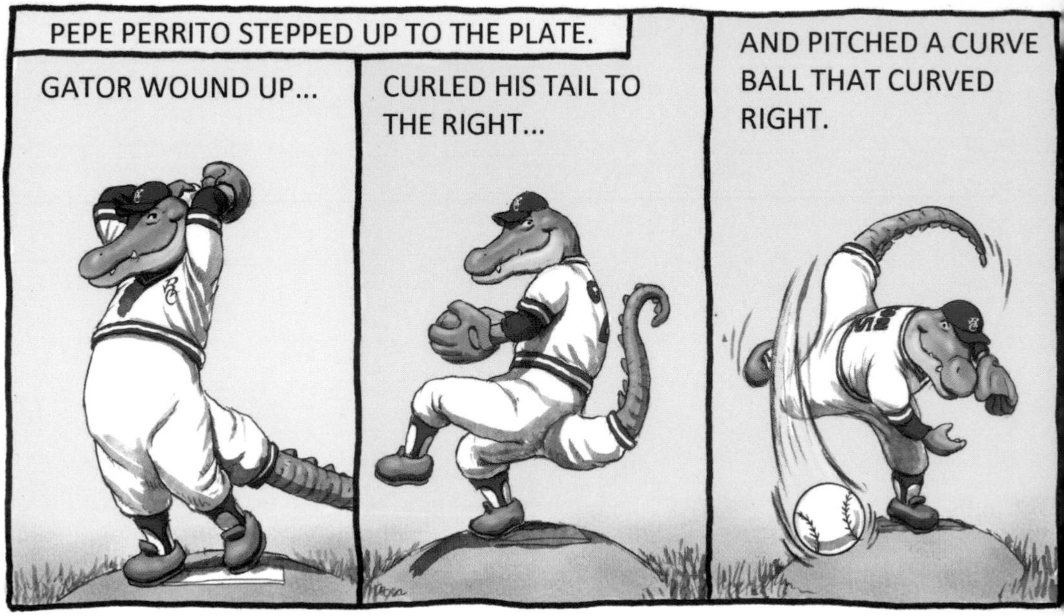
PEPE PERRITO STEPPED UP TO THE PLATE.
GATOR WOUND UP...
CURLED HIS TAIL TO THE RIGHT...
AND PITCHED A CURVE BALL THAT CURVED RIGHT.

PEPE KNEW JUST WHERE TO SWING AND...

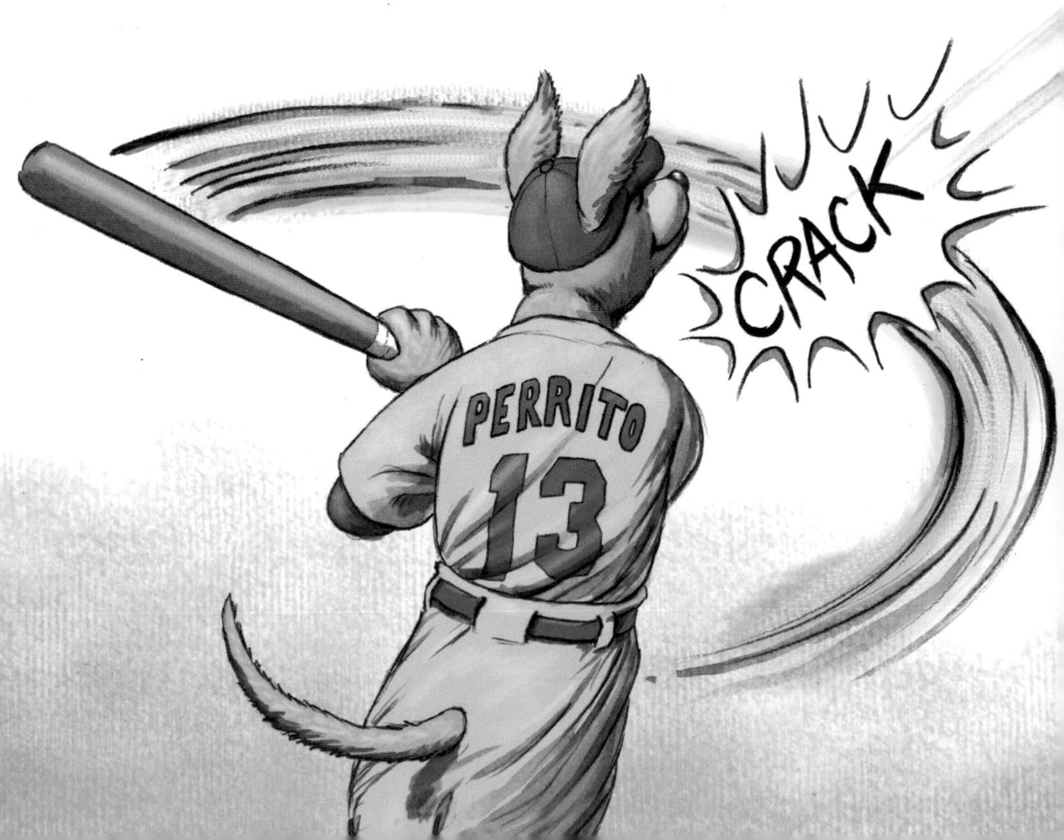
CRACK
PERRITO
13

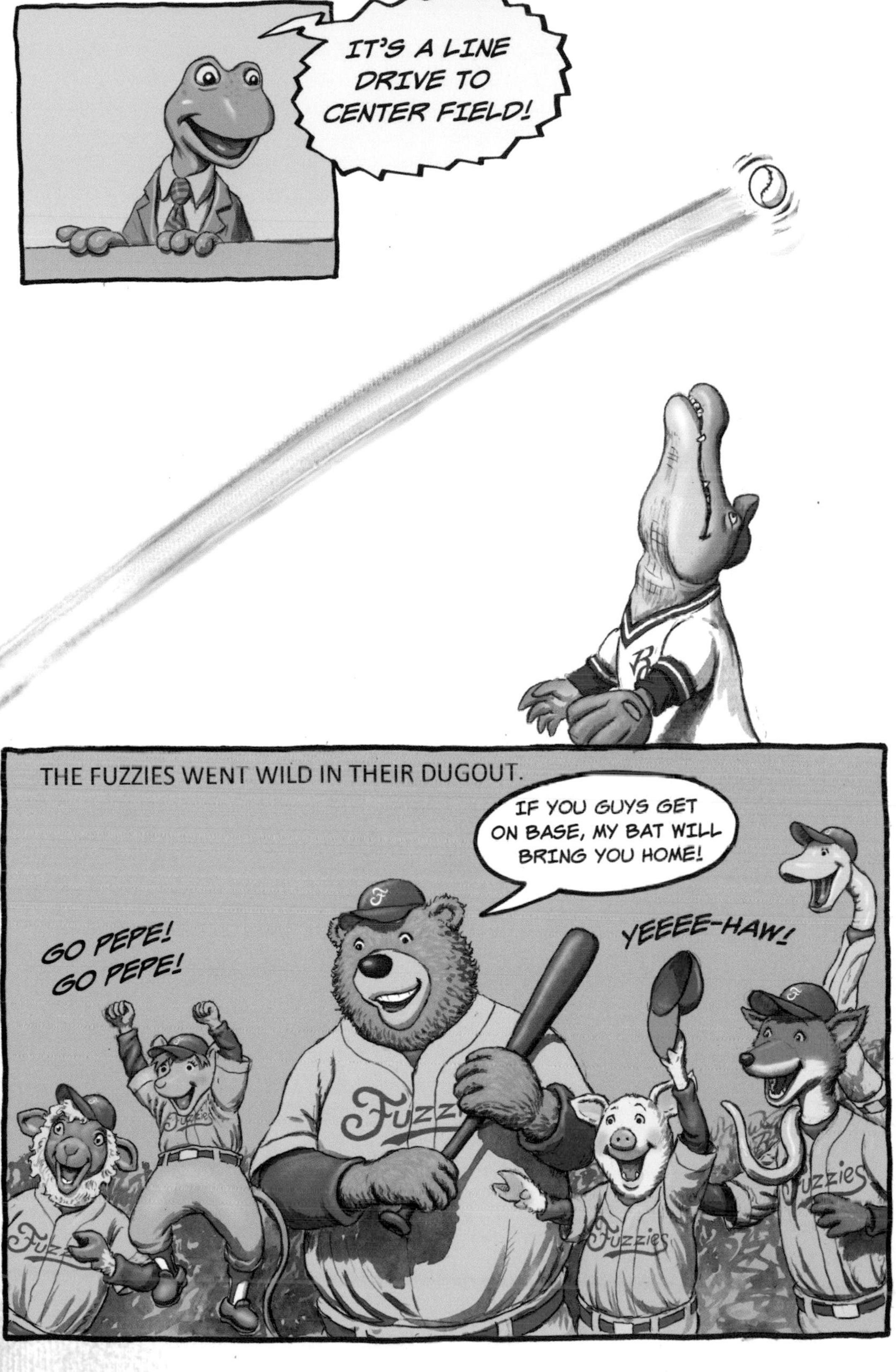
IT'S A LINE DRIVE TO CENTER FIELD!
THE FUZZIES WENT WILD IN THEIR DUGOUT.
GO PEPE! GO PEPE!
IF YOU GUYS GET ON BASE, MY BAT WILL BRING YOU HOME!
YEEEE-HAW!

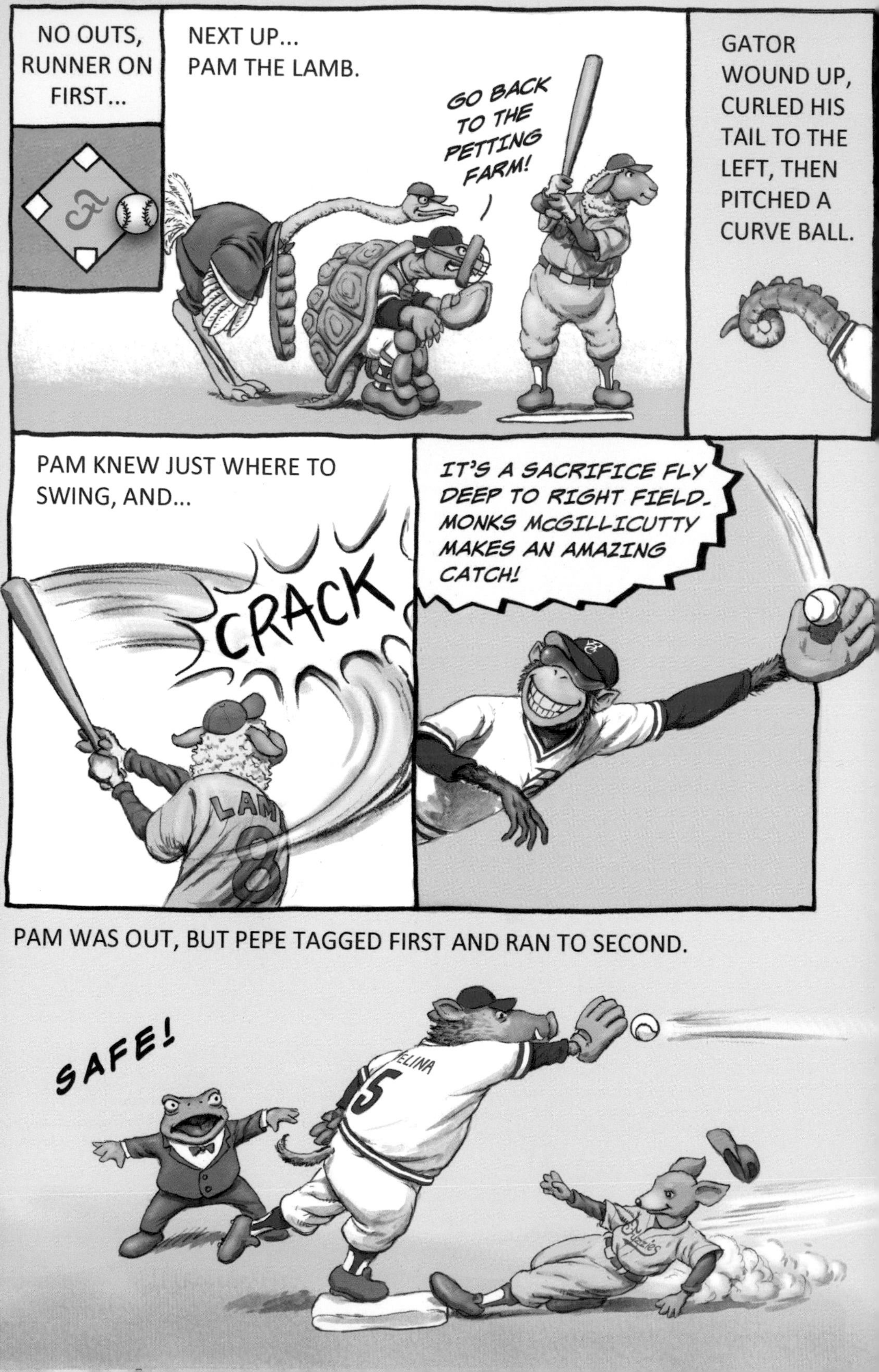
NO OUTS, RUNNER ON FIRST...
NEXT UP... PAM THE LAMB.
GO BACK TO THE PETTING FARM!
GATOR WOUND UP, CURLED HIS TAIL TO THE LEFT, THEN PITCHED A CURVE BALL.
PAM KNEW JUST WHERE TO SWING, AND...
CRACK
IT'S A SACRIFICE FLY DEEP TO RIGHT FIELD. MONKS McGILLICUTTY MAKES AN AMAZING CATCH!
PAM WAS OUT, BUT PEPE TAGGED FIRST AND RAN TO SECOND.
SAFE!

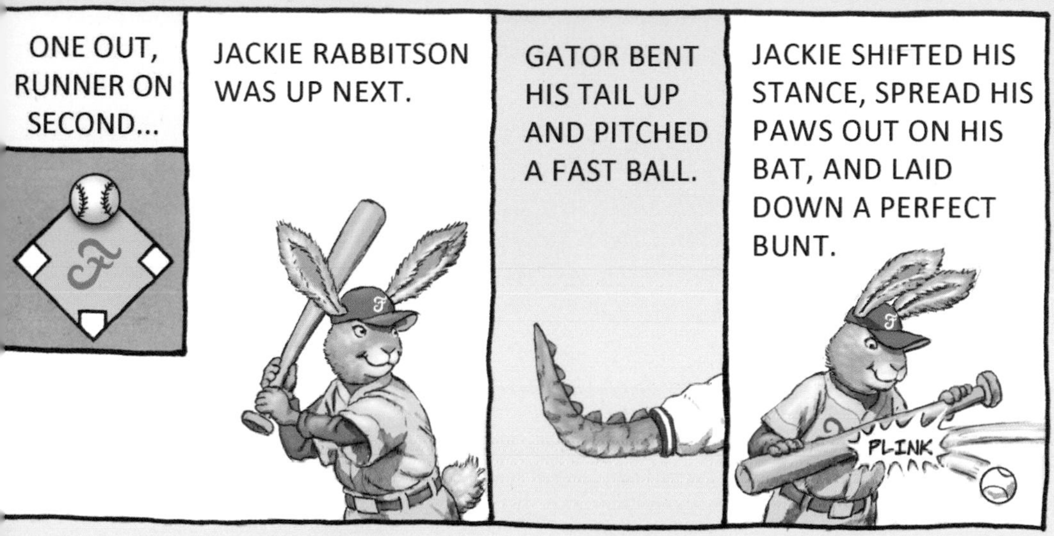
ONE OUT, RUNNER ON SECOND...
JACKIE RABBITSON WAS UP NEXT.
GATOR BENT HIS TAIL UP AND PITCHED A FAST BALL.
JACKIE SHIFTED HIS STANCE, SPREAD HIS PAWS OUT ON HIS BAT, AND LAID DOWN A PERFECT BUNT.
PLINK

RED CLAWS CATCHER "SNAPS" TORTELLI SCRAMBLED TO GET THE BALL AND THREW IT TO FIRST, BUT JACKIE WAS SAFE. AND PEPE RAN TO THIRD.

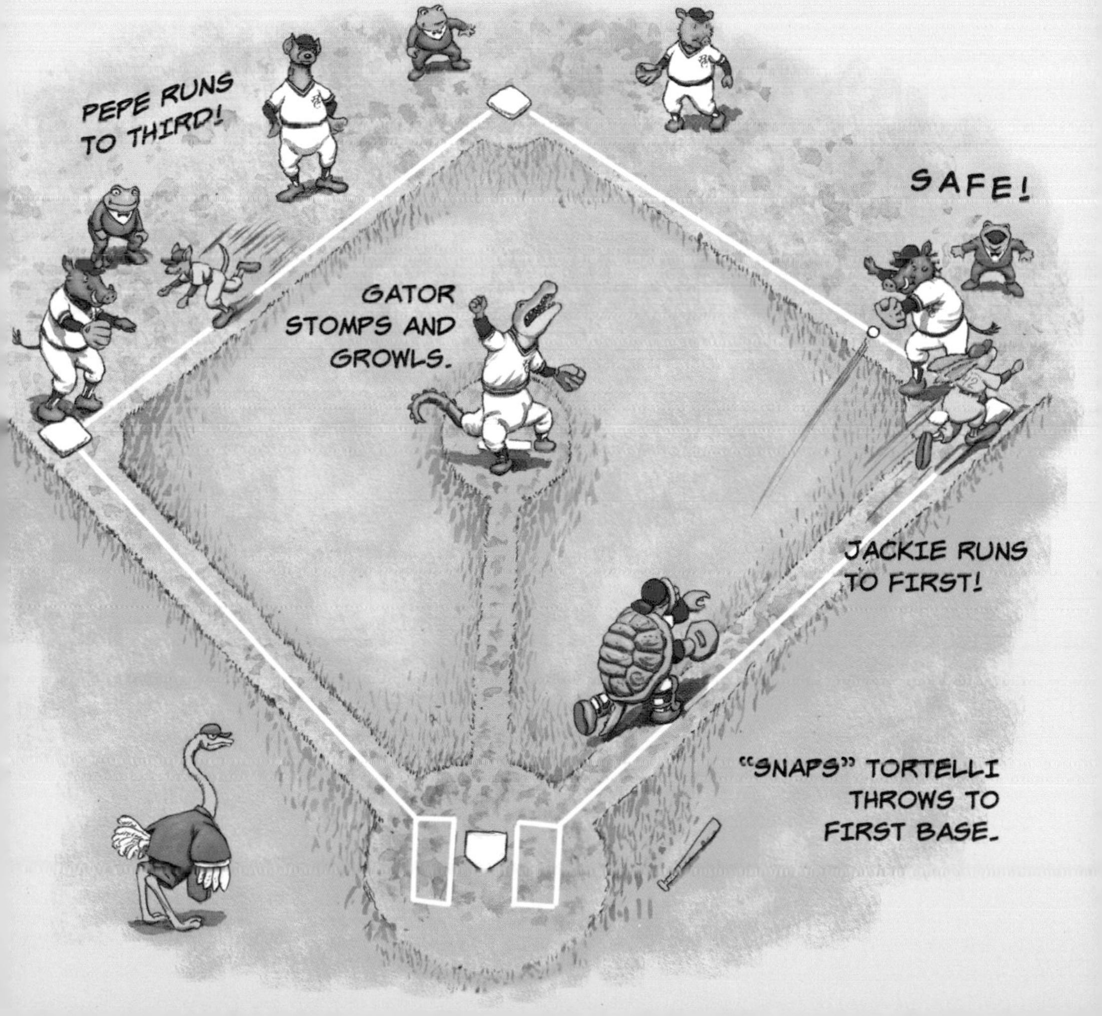
PEPE RUNS TO THIRD!
SAFE!
GATOR STOMPS AND GROWLS.
JACKIE RUNS TO FIRST!
"SNAPS" TORTELLI THROWS TO FIRST BASE.

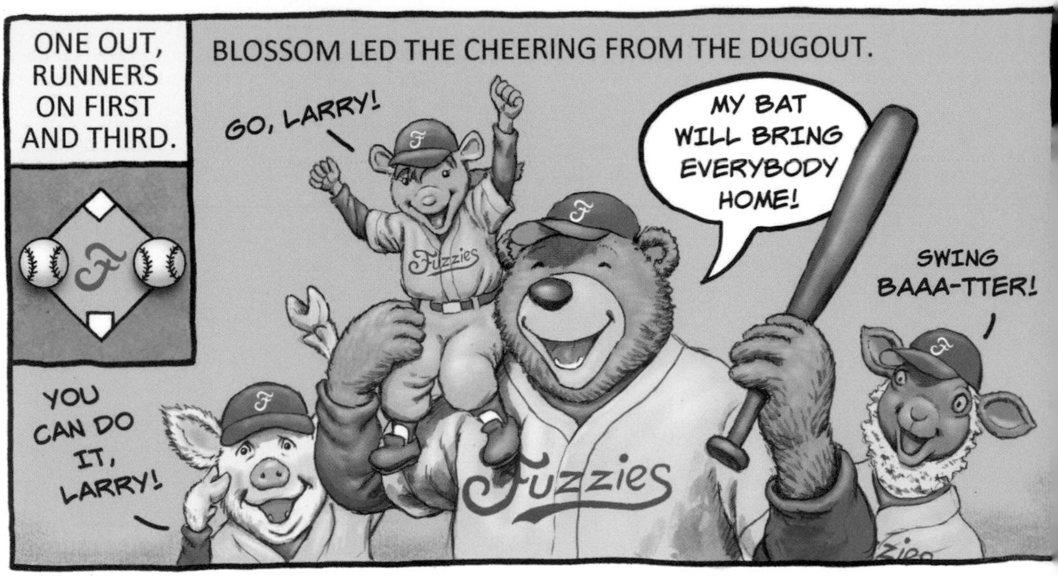
ONE OUT, RUNNERS ON FIRST AND THIRD.
BLOSSOM LED THE CHEERING FROM THE DUGOUT.
GO, LARRY!
MY BAT WILL BRING EVERYBODY HOME!
SWING BAAA-TTER!
YOU CAN DO IT, LARRY!
Fuzzies

LARRY BOA STEPPED UP TO THE PLATE. GATOR CURLED HIS TAIL TO THE LEFT AND PITCHED A CURVE BALL. LARRY DIDN'T SWING BUT...

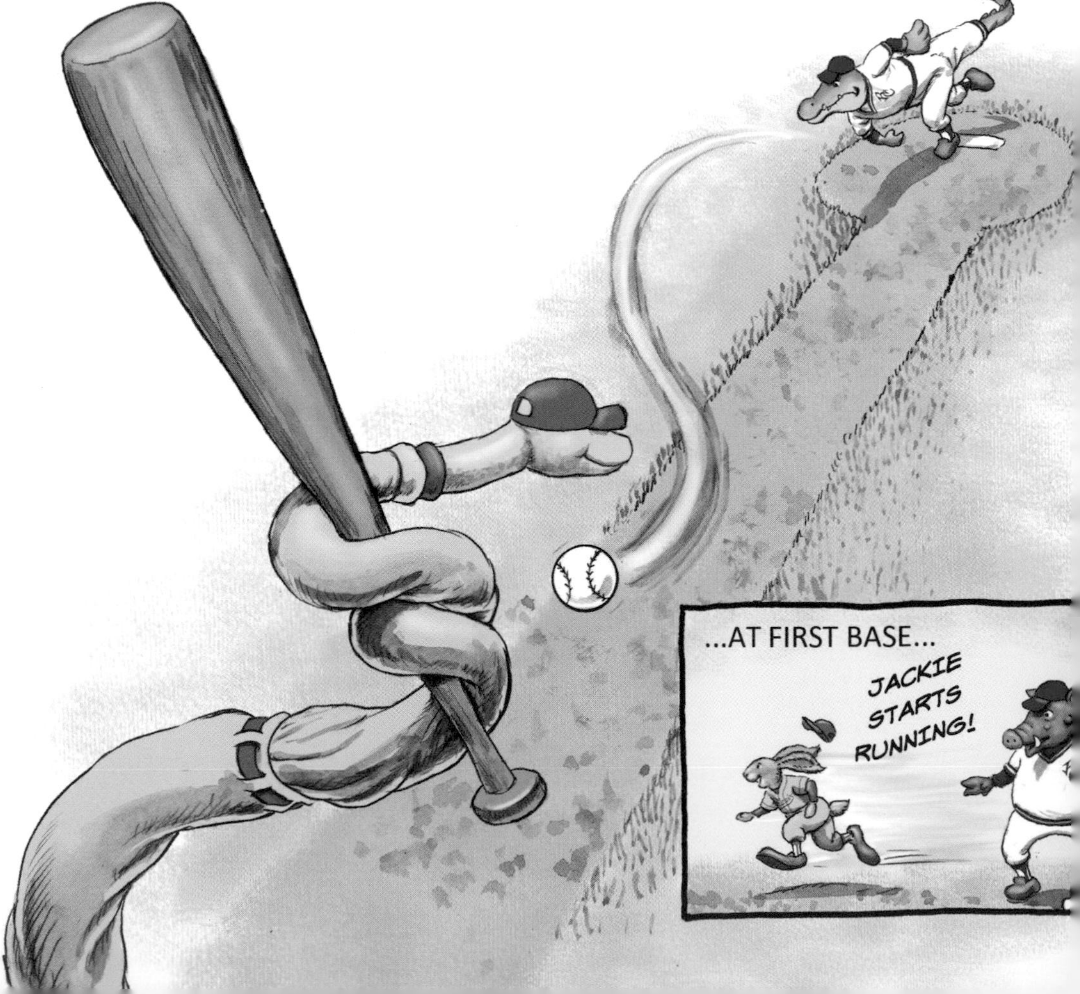
...AT FIRST BASE...
JACKIE STARTS RUNNING!

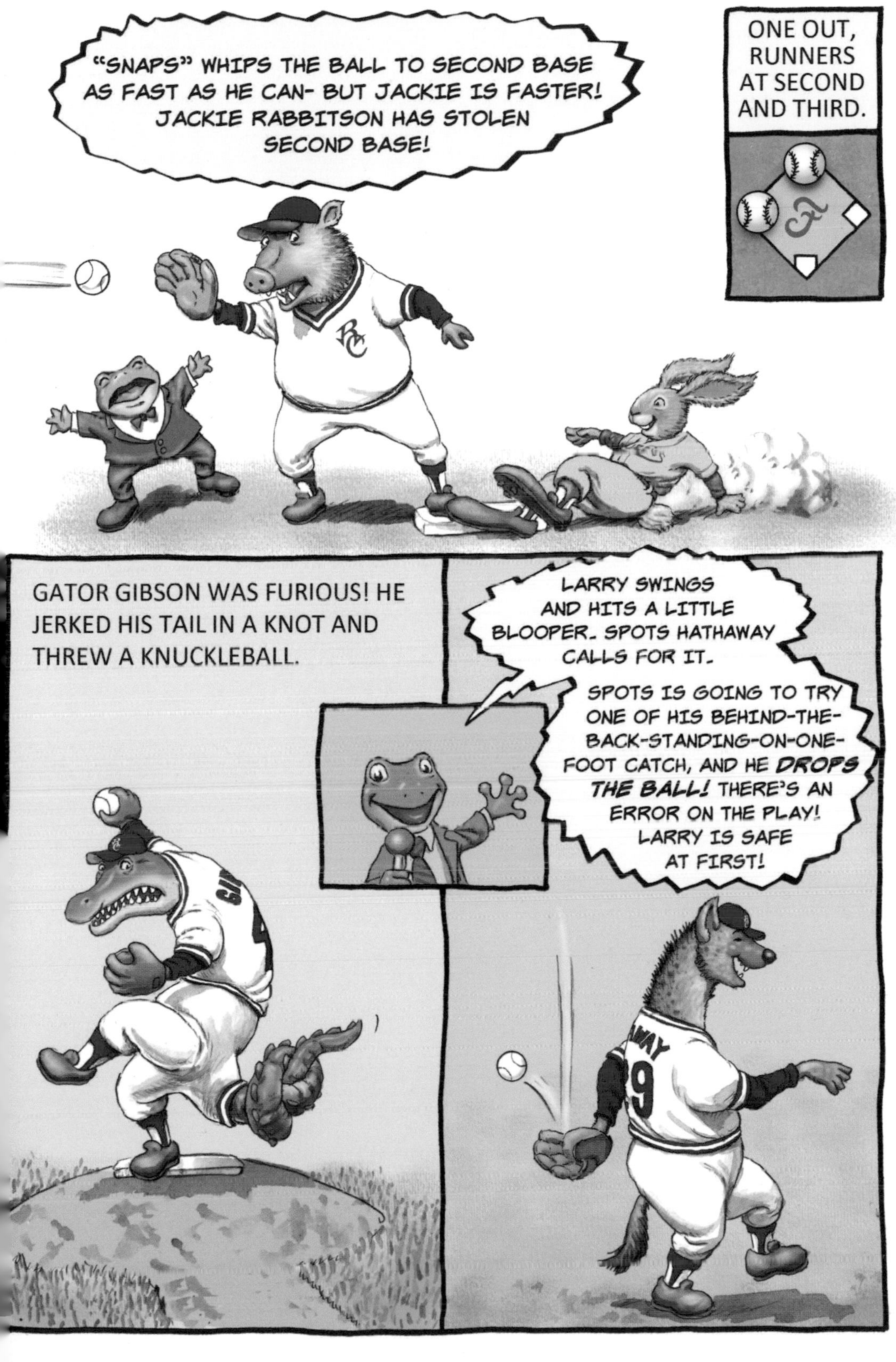
"SNAPS" WHIPS THE BALL TO SECOND BASE AS FAST AS HE CAN- BUT JACKIE IS FASTER! JACKIE RABBITSON HAS STOLEN SECOND BASE!
ONE OUT, RUNNERS AT SECOND AND THIRD.
GATOR GIBSON WAS FURIOUS! HE JERKED HIS TAIL IN A KNOT AND THREW A KNUCKLEBALL.
LARRY SWINGS AND HITS A LITTLE BLOOPER. SPOTS HATHAWAY CALLS FOR IT.
SPOTS IS GOING TO TRY ONE OF HIS BEHIND-THE-BACK-STANDING-ON-ONE-FOOT CATCH, AND HE *DROPS THE BALL!* THERE'S AN ERROR ON THE PLAY! LARRY IS SAFE AT FIRST!

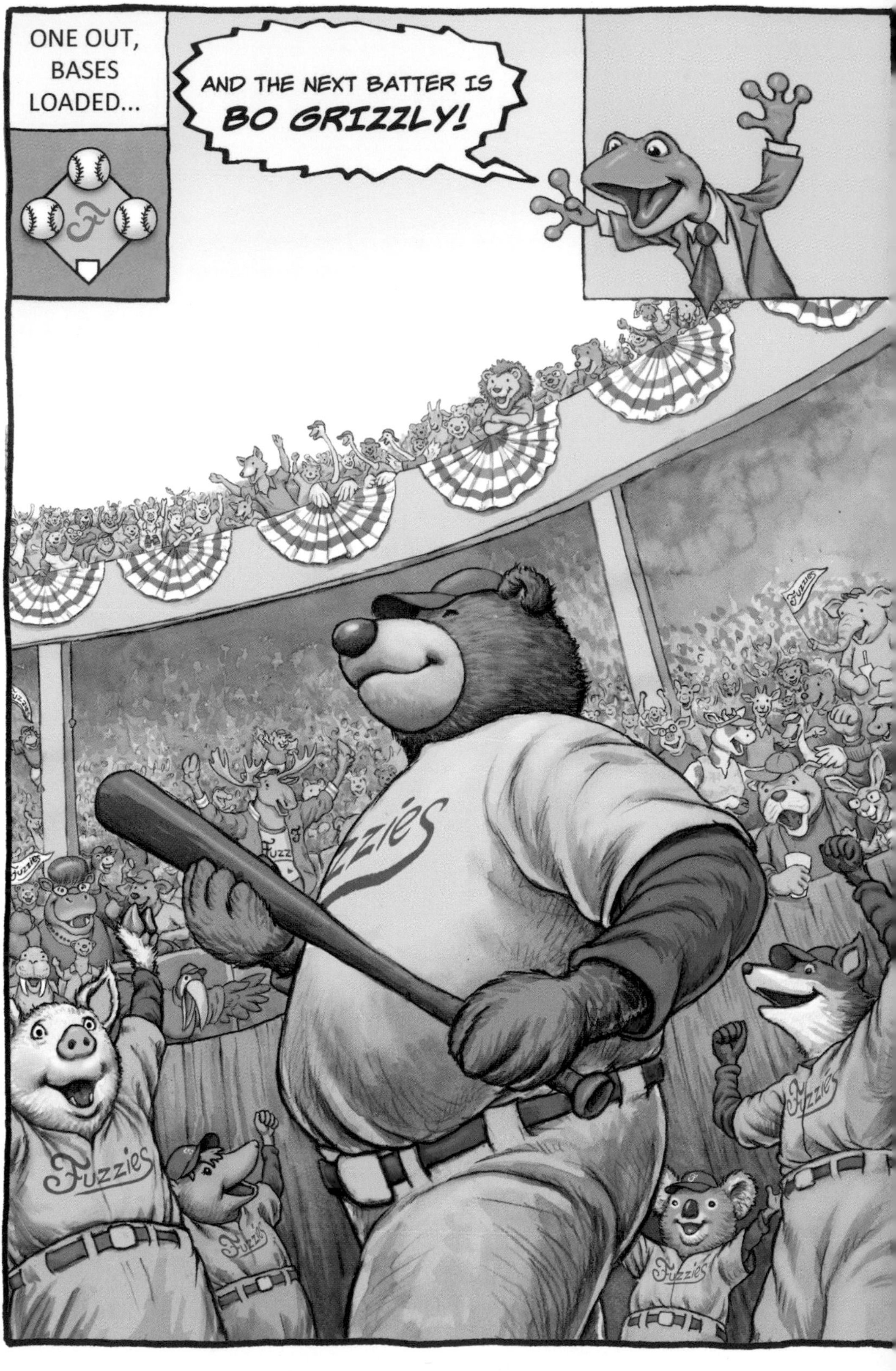
ONE OUT, BASES LOADED...
AND THE NEXT BATTER IS BO GRIZZLY!
Fuzzies

RED CLAWS MANAGER MITZI McGRAW WALKED OUT TO THE MOUND.

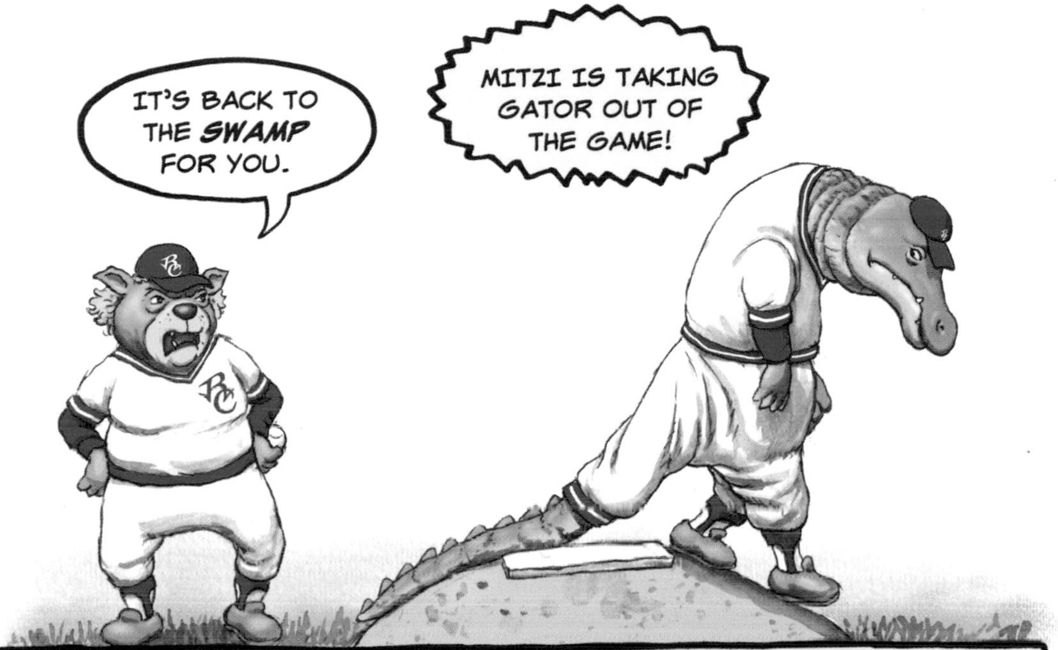
IT'S BACK TO THE SWAMP FOR YOU.
MITZI IS TAKING GATOR OUT OF THE GAME!

MITZI SIGNALED TO THE BULL PEN. RED CLAWS STAR RELIEF PITCHER, FERNANDO DEL TORO, CHARGED TO THE MOUND.

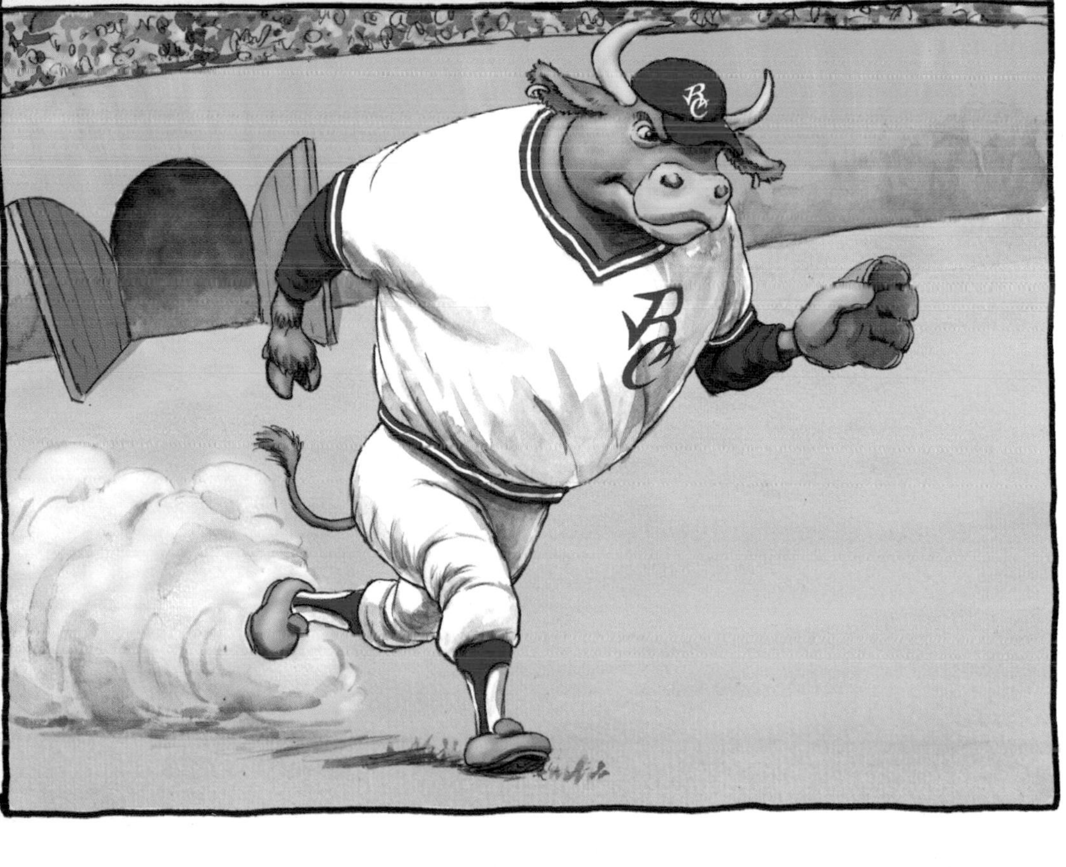

THE FUZZY'S DUGOUT WAS SUDDENLY SILENT AGAIN.

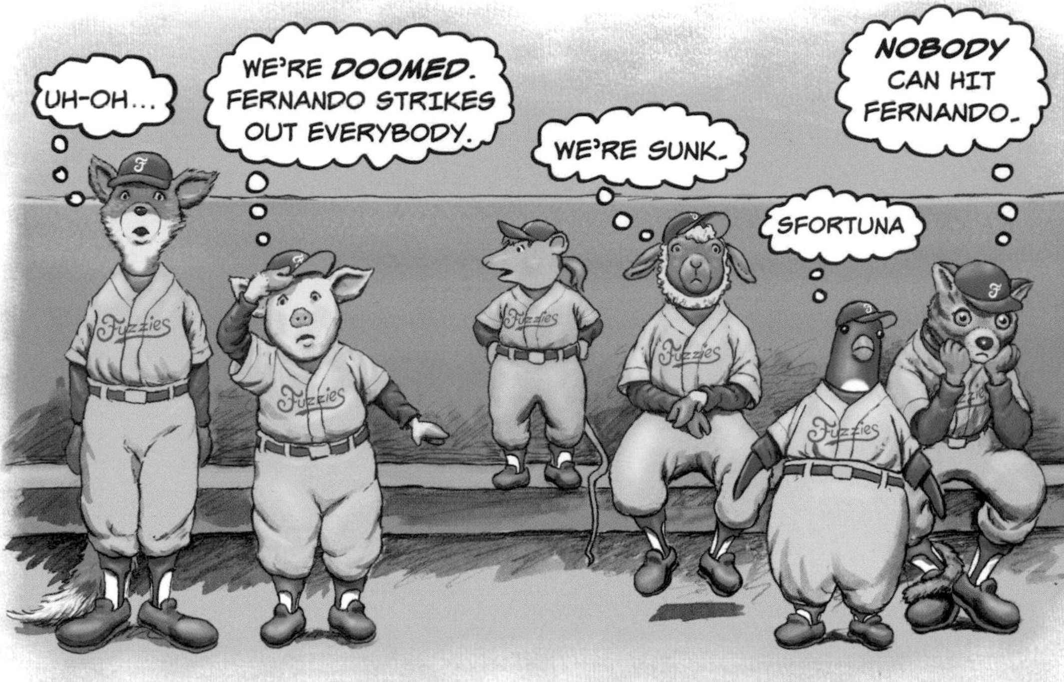
UH-OH...
WE'RE DOOMED. FERNANDO STRIKES OUT EVERYBODY.
WE'RE SUNK.
SFORTUNA
NOBODY CAN HIT FERNANDO.

BLOSSOM COULD NOT STAY QUIET... AND NEITHER COULD ANYBODY ELSE!

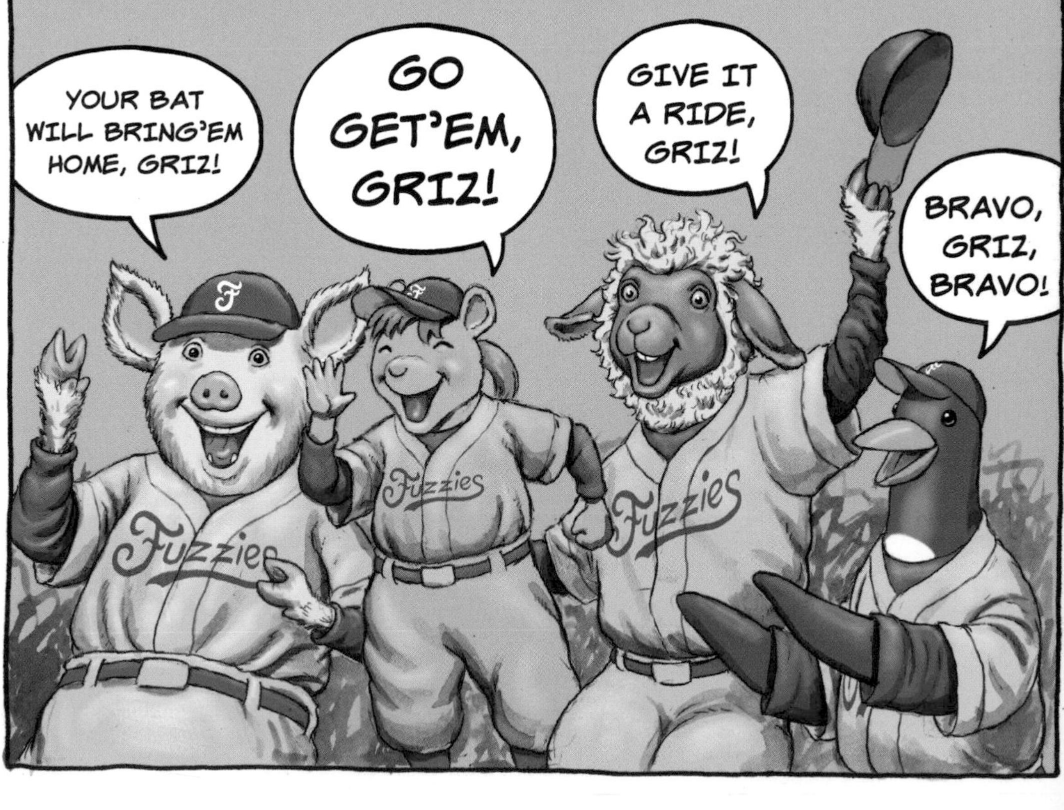
YOUR BAT WILL BRING'EM HOME, GRIZ!
GO GET'EM, GRIZ!
GIVE IT A RIDE, GRIZ!
BRAVO, GRIZ, BRAVO!

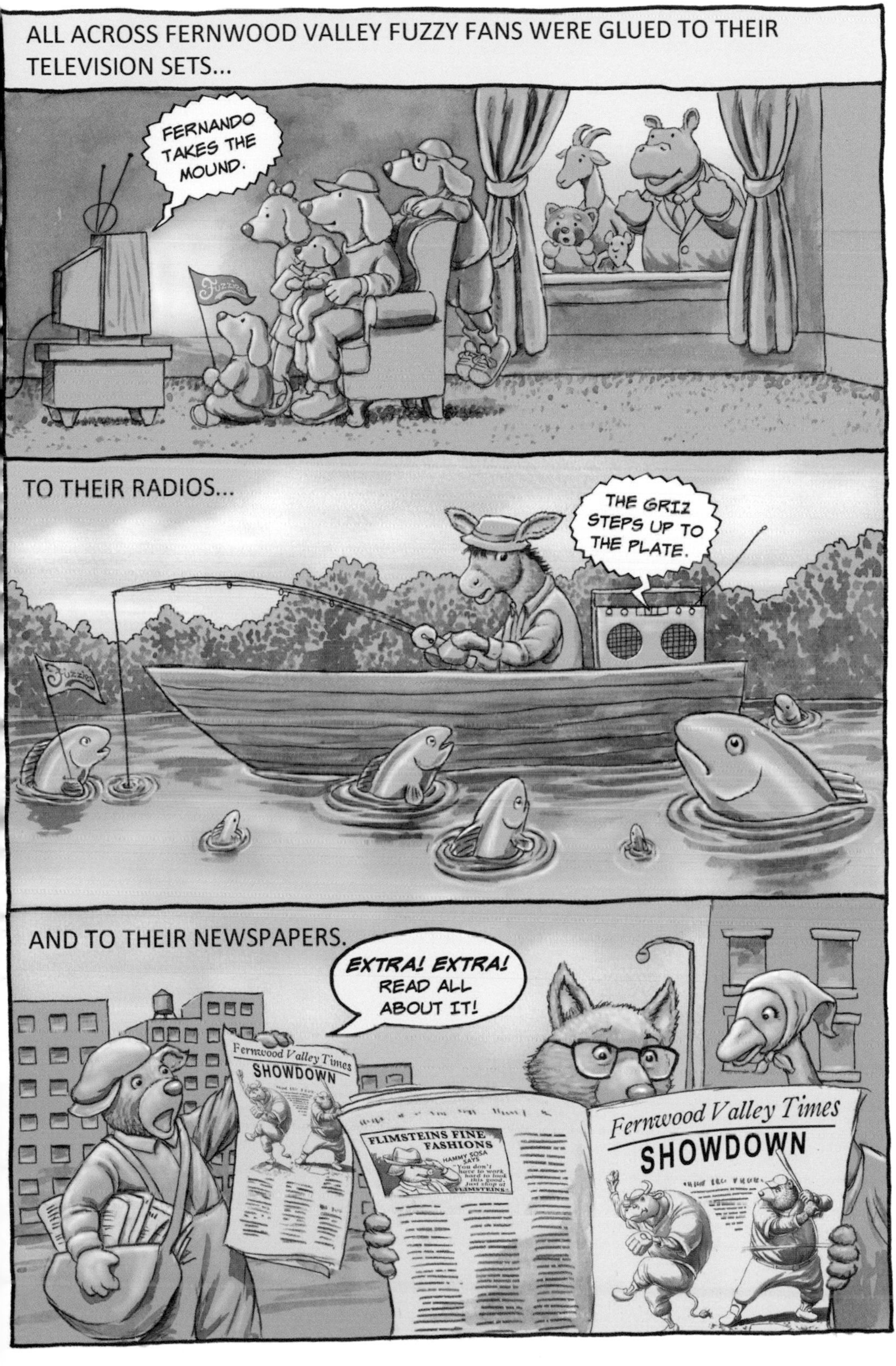

ALL ACROSS FERNWOOD VALLEY FUZZY FANS WERE GLUED TO THEIR TELEVISION SETS...
FERNANDO TAKES THE MOUND.
TO THEIR RADIOS...
THE GRIZ STEPS UP TO THE PLATE.
AND TO THEIR NEWSPAPERS.
EXTRA! EXTRA! READ ALL ABOUT IT!
Fernwood Valley Times
SHOWDOWN
FLIMSTEINS FINE FASHIONS
HAMMY SOSA SAYS
Fernwood Valley Times
SHOWDOWN

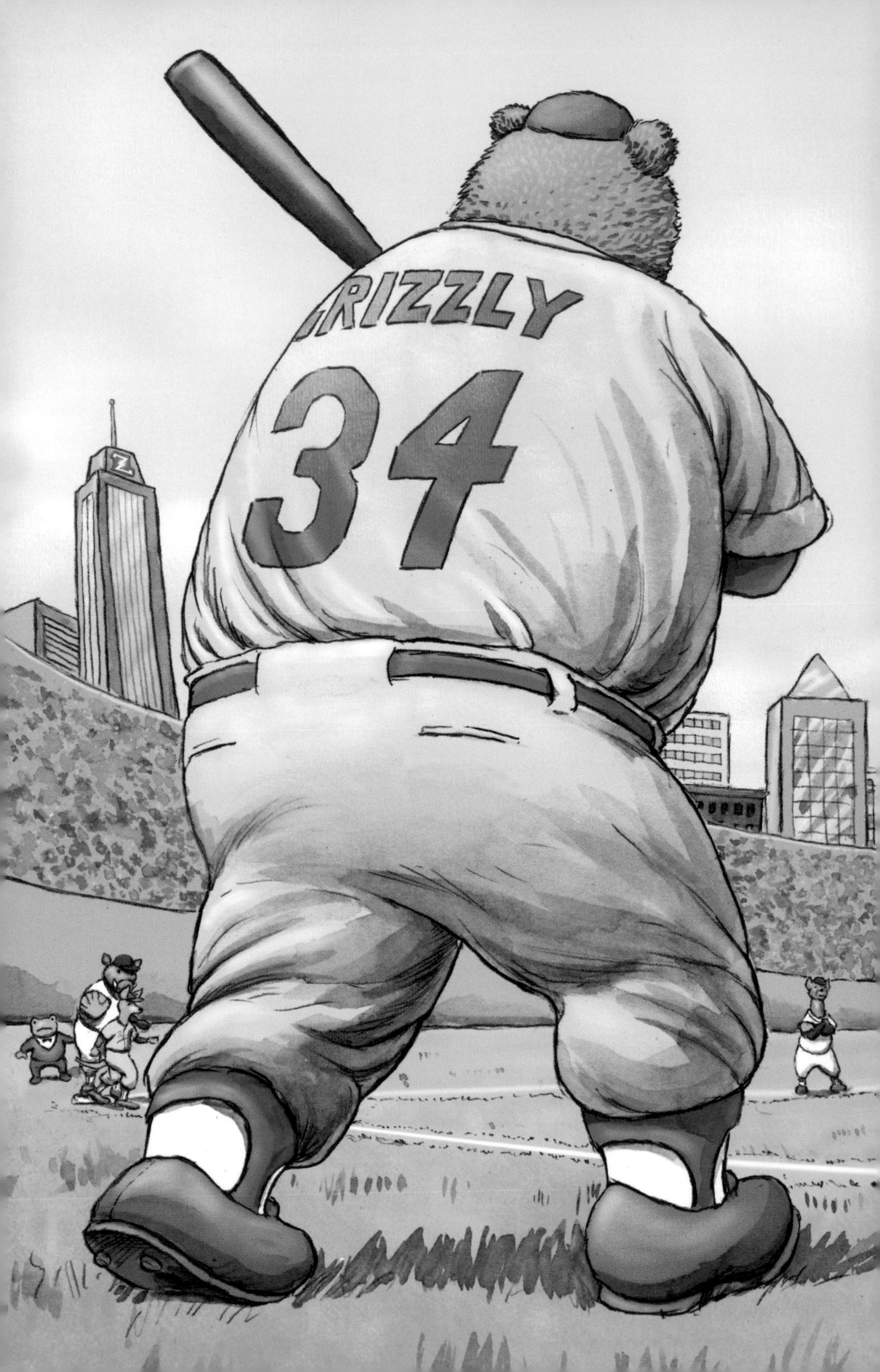
GRIZZLY
34

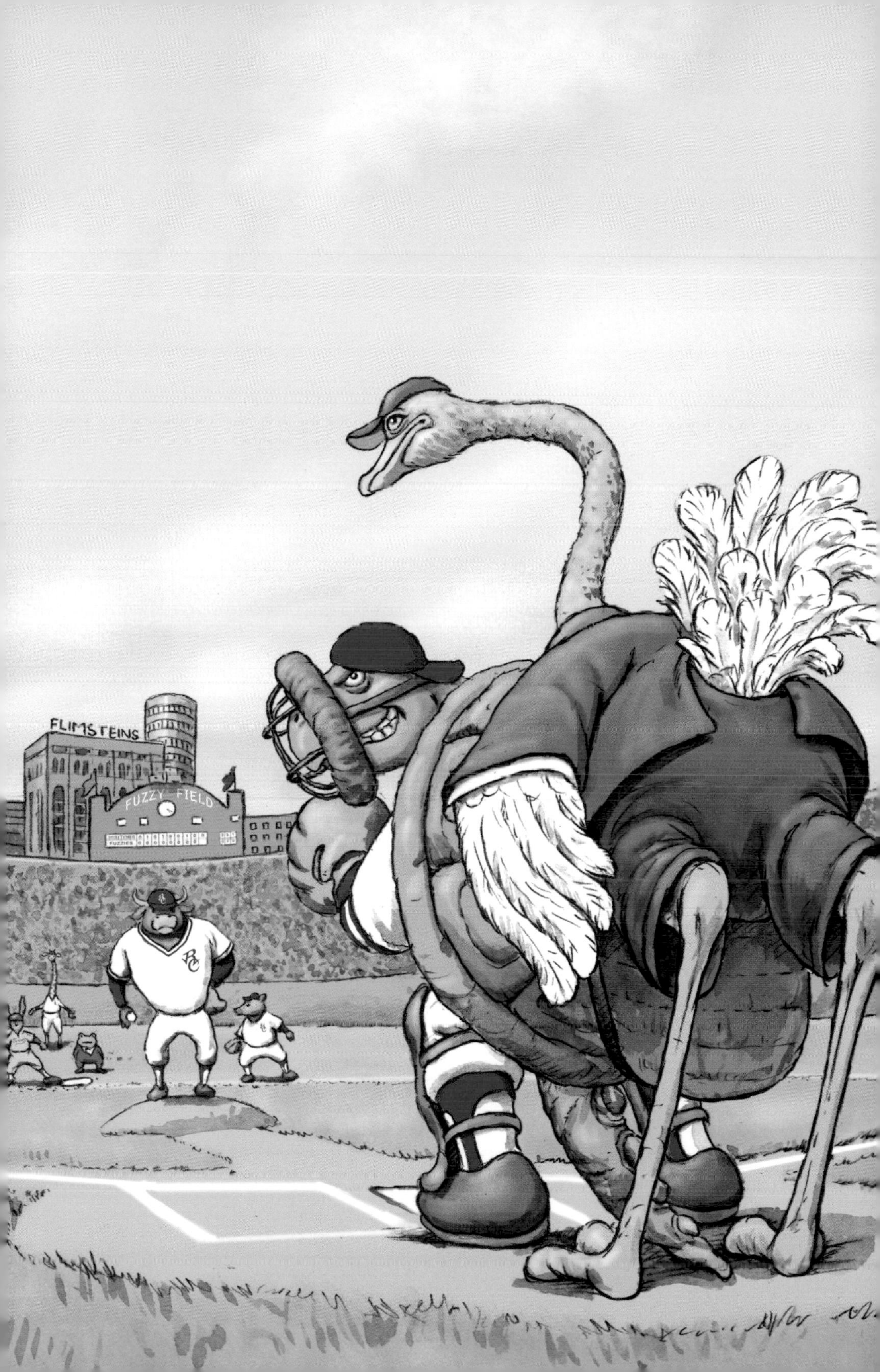
FLIMSTEINS
FUZZY FIELD

FOUR TIMES FERNANDO SNORTED, STOMPED HIS FOOT, WOUND UP, AND THREW A LIGHTNING FAST PITCH.

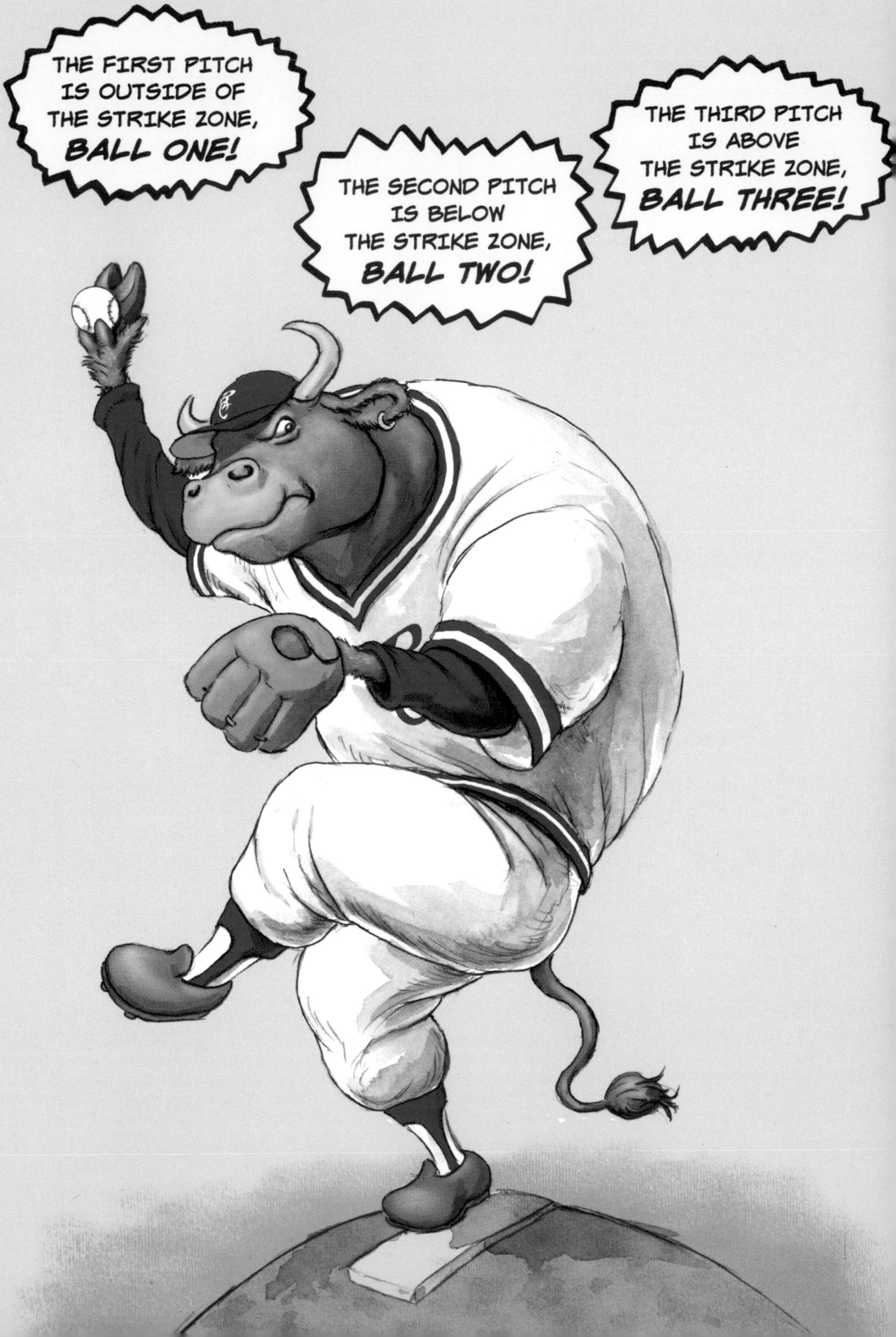

THE FIRST PITCH IS OUTSIDE OF THE STRIKE ZONE, **BALL ONE!**
THE SECOND PITCH IS BELOW THE STRIKE ZONE, **BALL TWO!**
THE THIRD PITCH IS ABOVE THE STRIKE ZONE, **BALL THREE!**

AND FOUR TIMES THE GRIZ DID NOT SWING. HE DID NOT TWITCH. HE DID NOT EVEN BLINK.

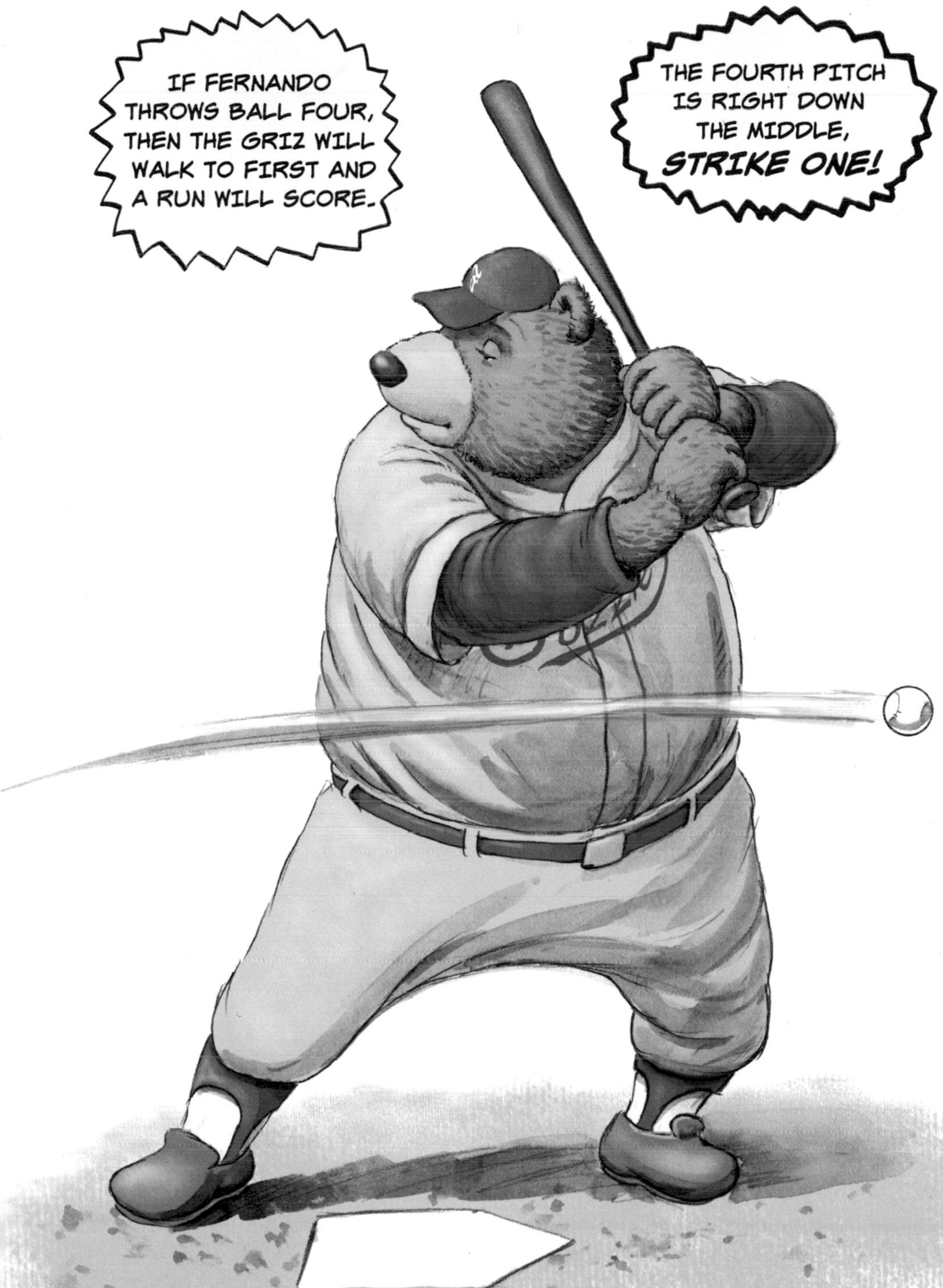
IF FERNANDO THROWS BALL FOUR, THEN THE GRIZ WILL WALK TO FIRST AND A RUN WILL SCORE.
THE FOURTH PITCH IS RIGHT DOWN THE MIDDLE, STRIKE ONE!

THREE BALLS AND ONE STRIKE. FERNANDO WOUND UP AND THREW A FASTBAL
DOWN THE MIDDLE OF THE PLATE. THE GRIZ TOOK A BIG SWING AND...

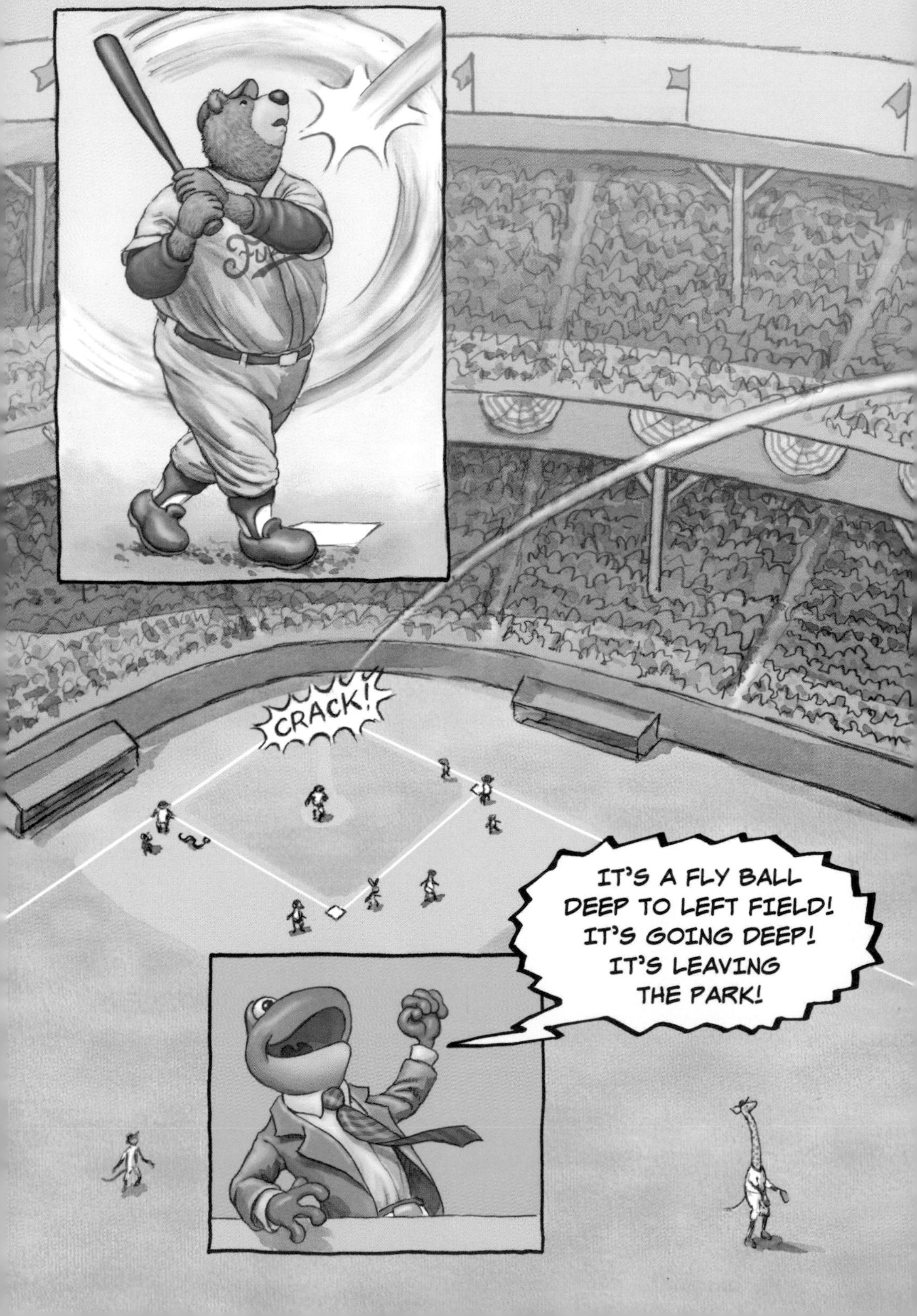
CRACK!
IT'S A FLY BALL DEEP TO LEFT FIELD! IT'S GOING DEEP! IT'S LEAVING THE PARK!

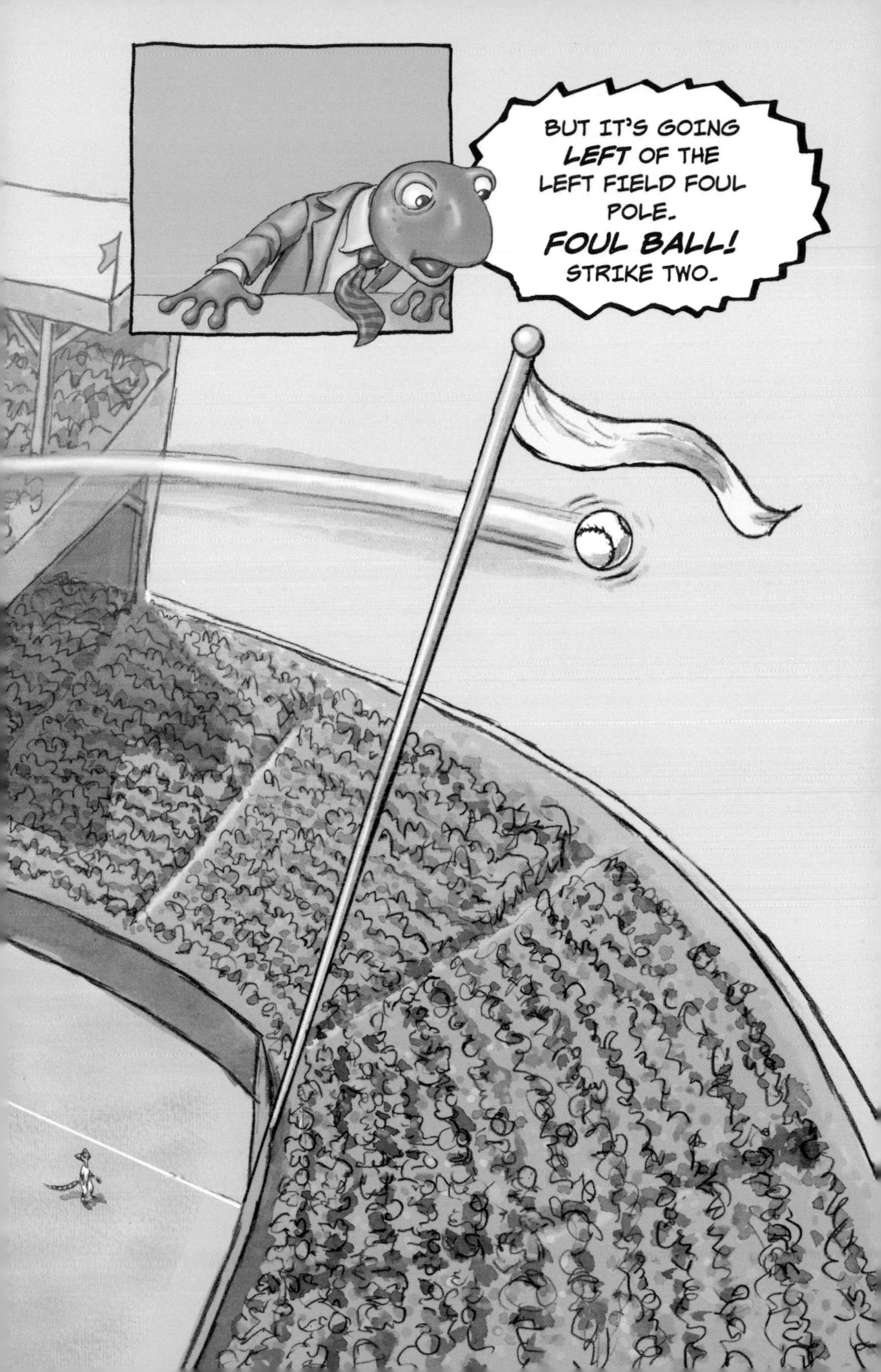
BUT IT'S GOING **LEFT** OF THE LEFT FIELD FOUL POLE. **FOUL BALL!** STRIKE TWO.

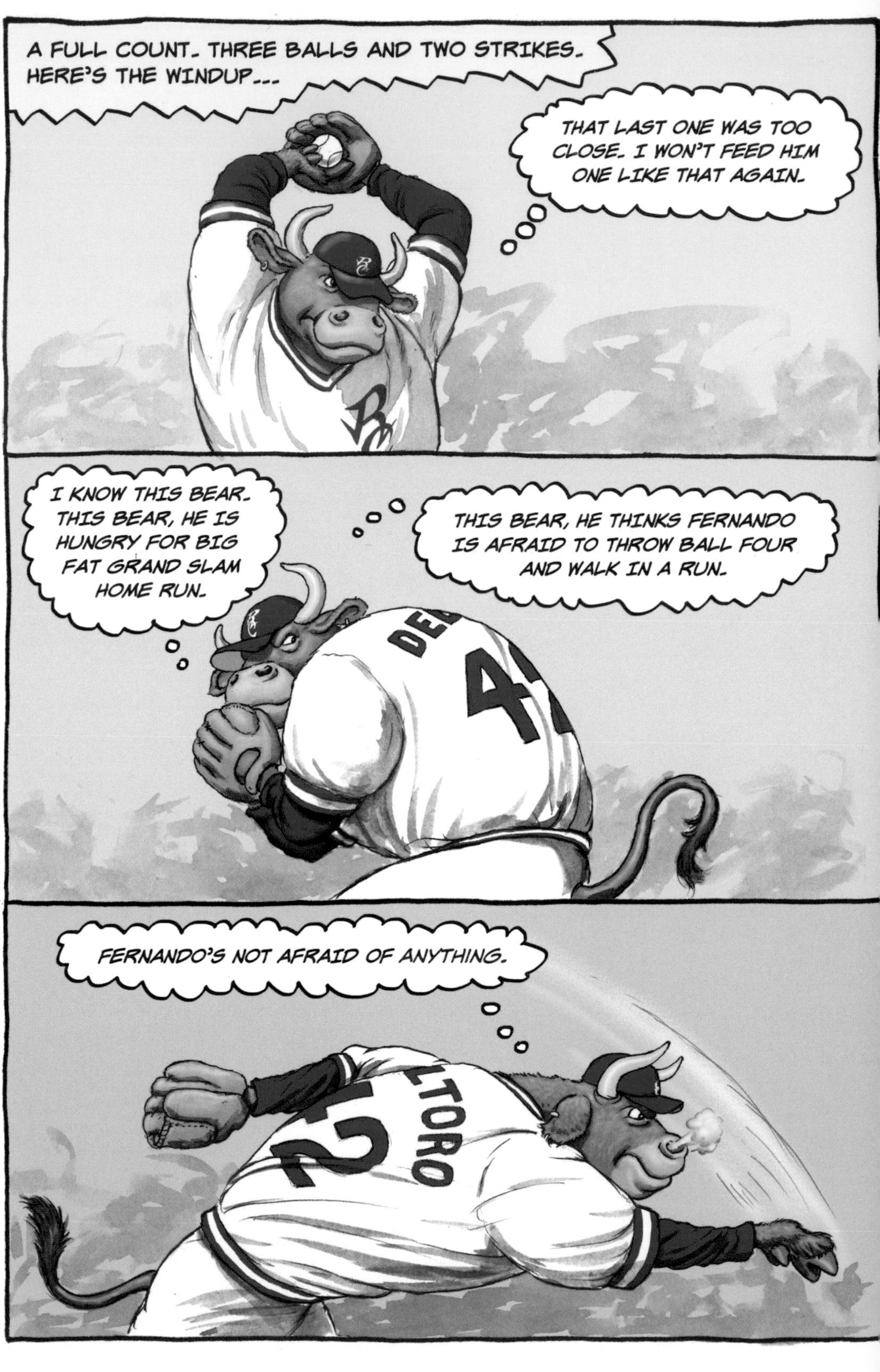
A FULL COUNT. THREE BALLS AND TWO STRIKES. HERE'S THE WINDUP...
THAT LAST ONE WAS TOO CLOSE. I WON'T FEED HIM ONE LIKE THAT AGAIN.
I KNOW THIS BEAR. THIS BEAR, HE IS HUNGRY FOR BIG FAT GRAND SLAM HOME RUN.
THIS BEAR, HE THINKS FERNANDO IS AFRAID TO THROW BALL FOUR AND WALK IN A RUN.
FERNANDO'S NOT AFRAID OF ANYTHING.

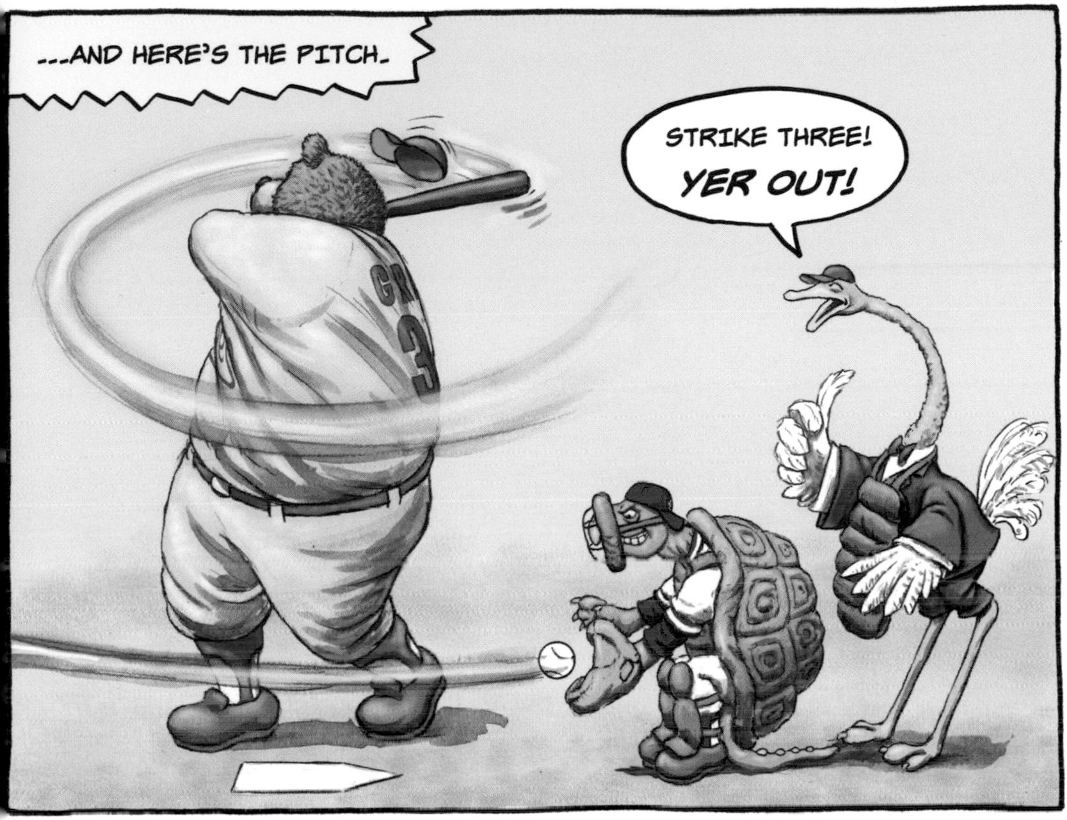
...AND HERE'S THE PITCH.
STRIKE THREE! YER OUT!

THERE WAS NO JOY IN FERNWOOD VALLEY.

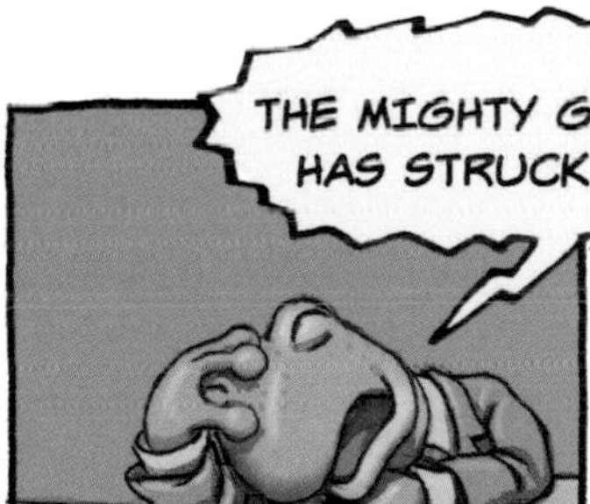
THE MIGHTY GRIZZLY HAS STRUCK OUT.

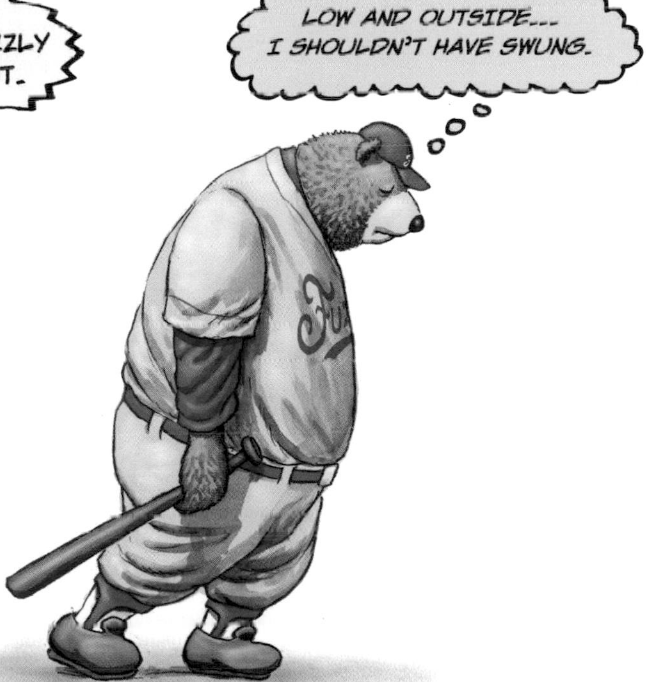
LOW AND OUTSIDE... I SHOULDN'T HAVE SWUNG.

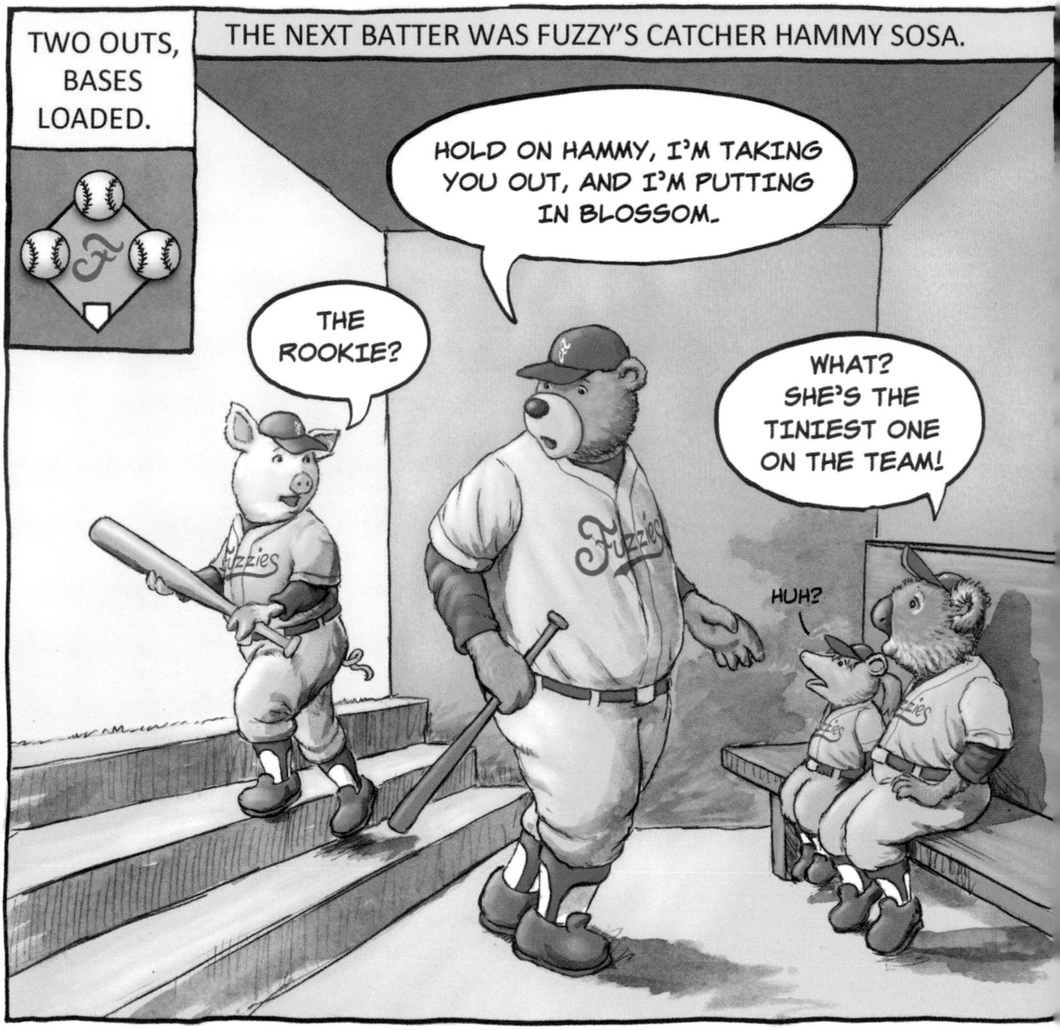
TWO OUTS, BASES LOADED.
THE NEXT BATTER WAS FUZZY'S CATCHER HAMMY SOSA.
HOLD ON HAMMY, I'M TAKING YOU OUT, AND I'M PUTTING IN BLOSSOM.
THE ROOKIE?
WHAT? SHE'S THE TINIEST ONE ON THE TEAM!
HUH?

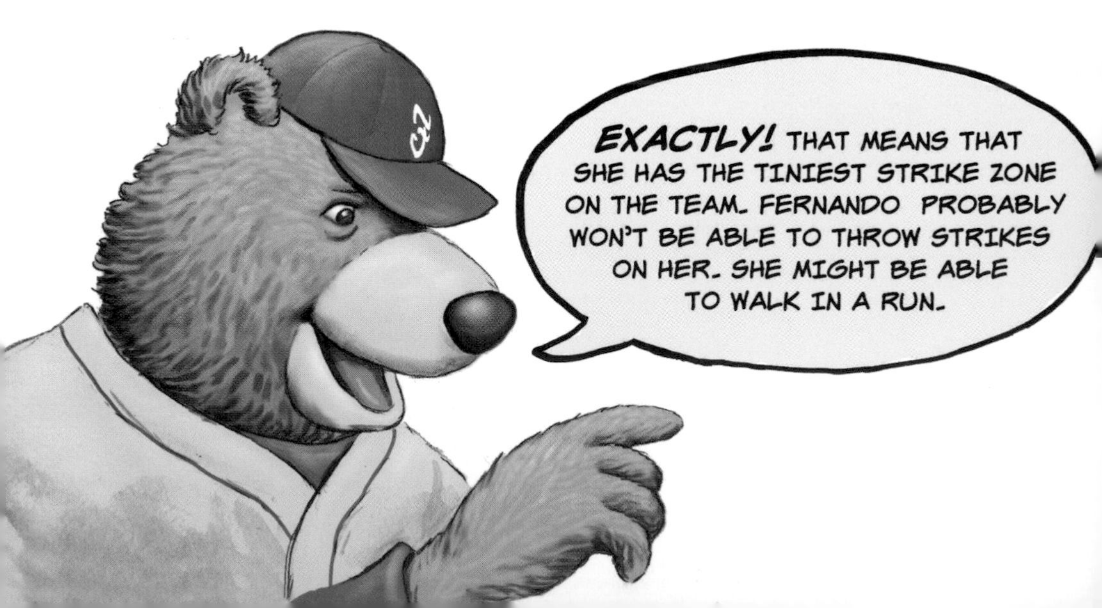
EXACTLY! THAT MEANS THAT SHE HAS THE TINIEST STRIKE ZONE ON THE TEAM. FERNANDO PROBABLY WON'T BE ABLE TO THROW STRIKES ON HER. SHE MIGHT BE ABLE TO WALK IN A RUN.

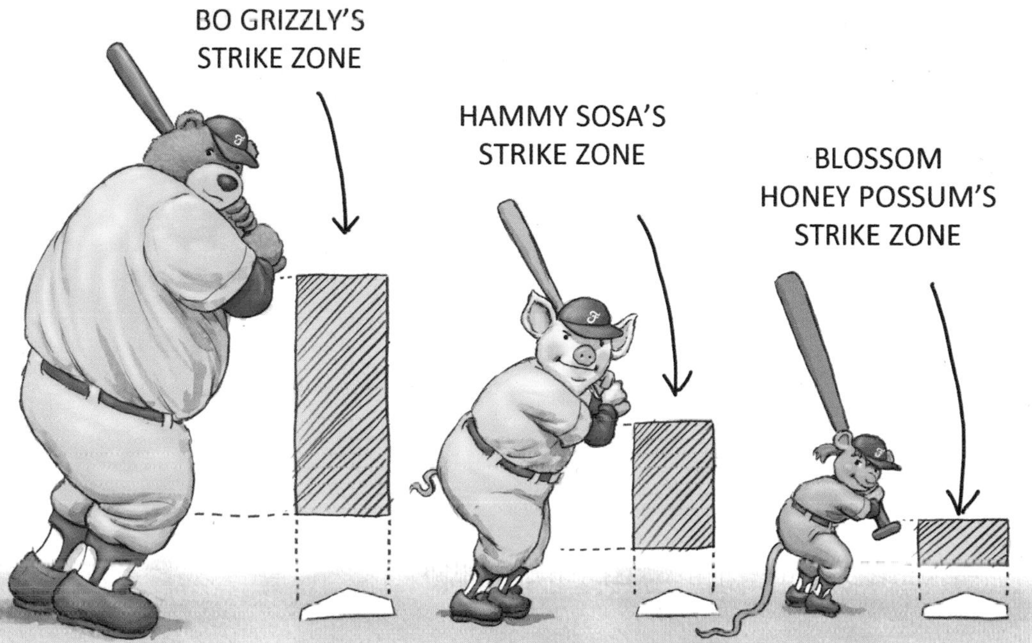
BO GRIZZLY'S STRIKE ZONE
HAMMY SOSA'S STRIKE ZONE
BLOSSOM HONEY POSSUM'S STRIKE ZONE

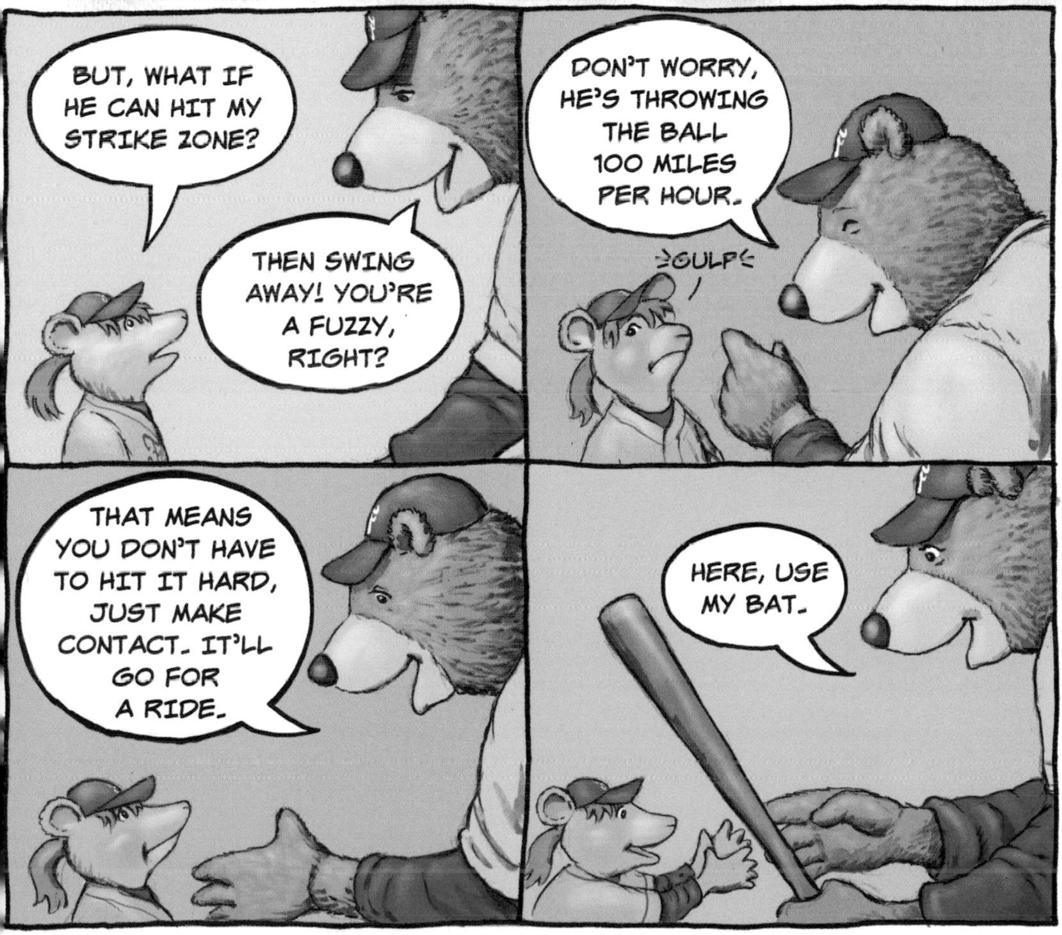
BUT, WHAT IF HE CAN HIT MY STRIKE ZONE?
THEN SWING AWAY! YOU'RE A FUZZY, RIGHT?
DON'T WORRY, HE'S THROWING THE BALL 100 MILES PER HOUR.
GULP
THAT MEANS YOU DON'T HAVE TO HIT IT HARD, JUST MAKE CONTACT. IT'LL GO FOR A RIDE.
HERE, USE MY BAT.

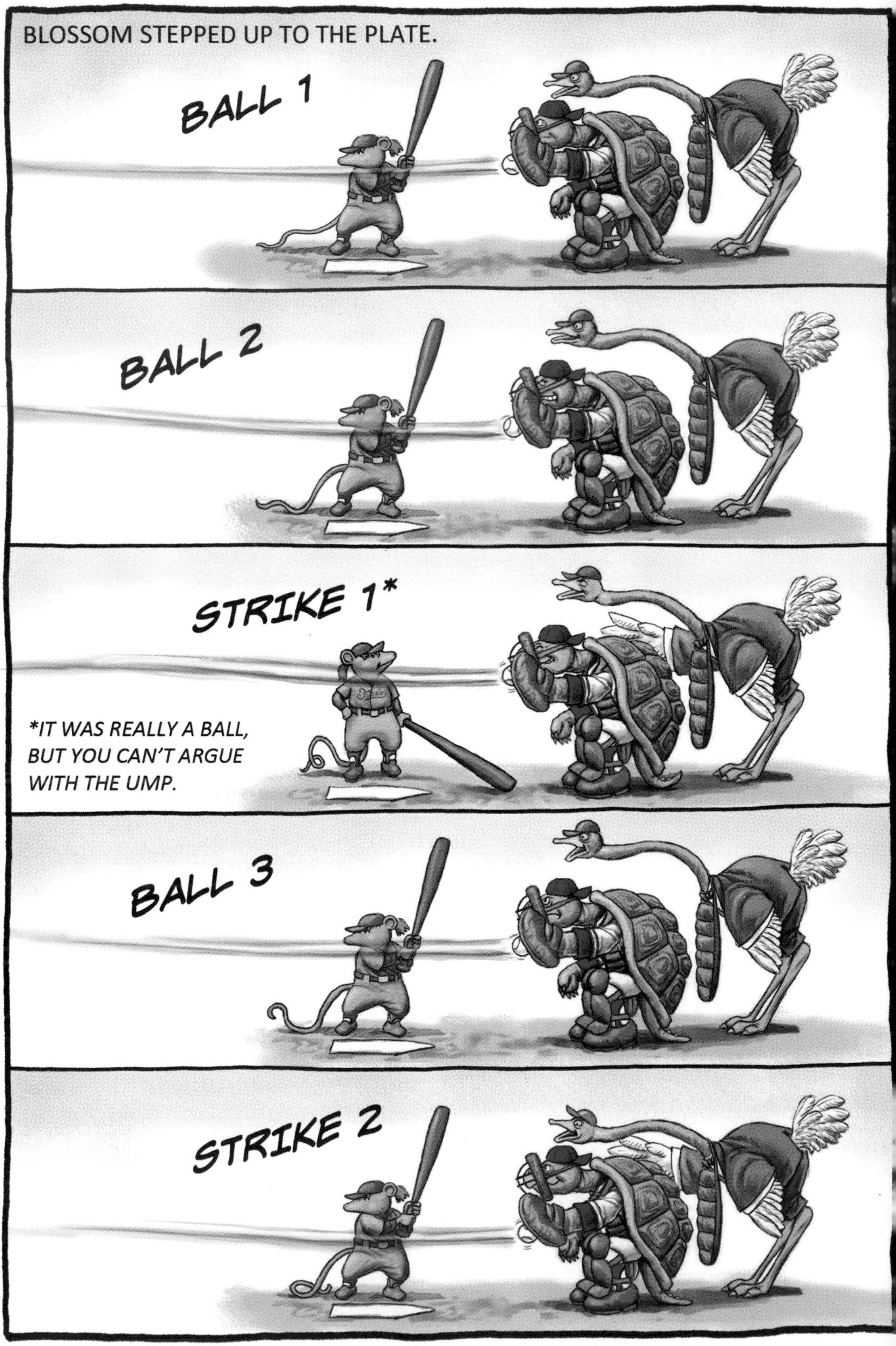
BLOSSOM STEPPED UP TO THE PLATE.
BALL 1
BALL 2
STRIKE 1*
*IT WAS REALLY A BALL, BUT YOU CAN'T ARGUE WITH THE UMP.
BALL 3
STRIKE 2

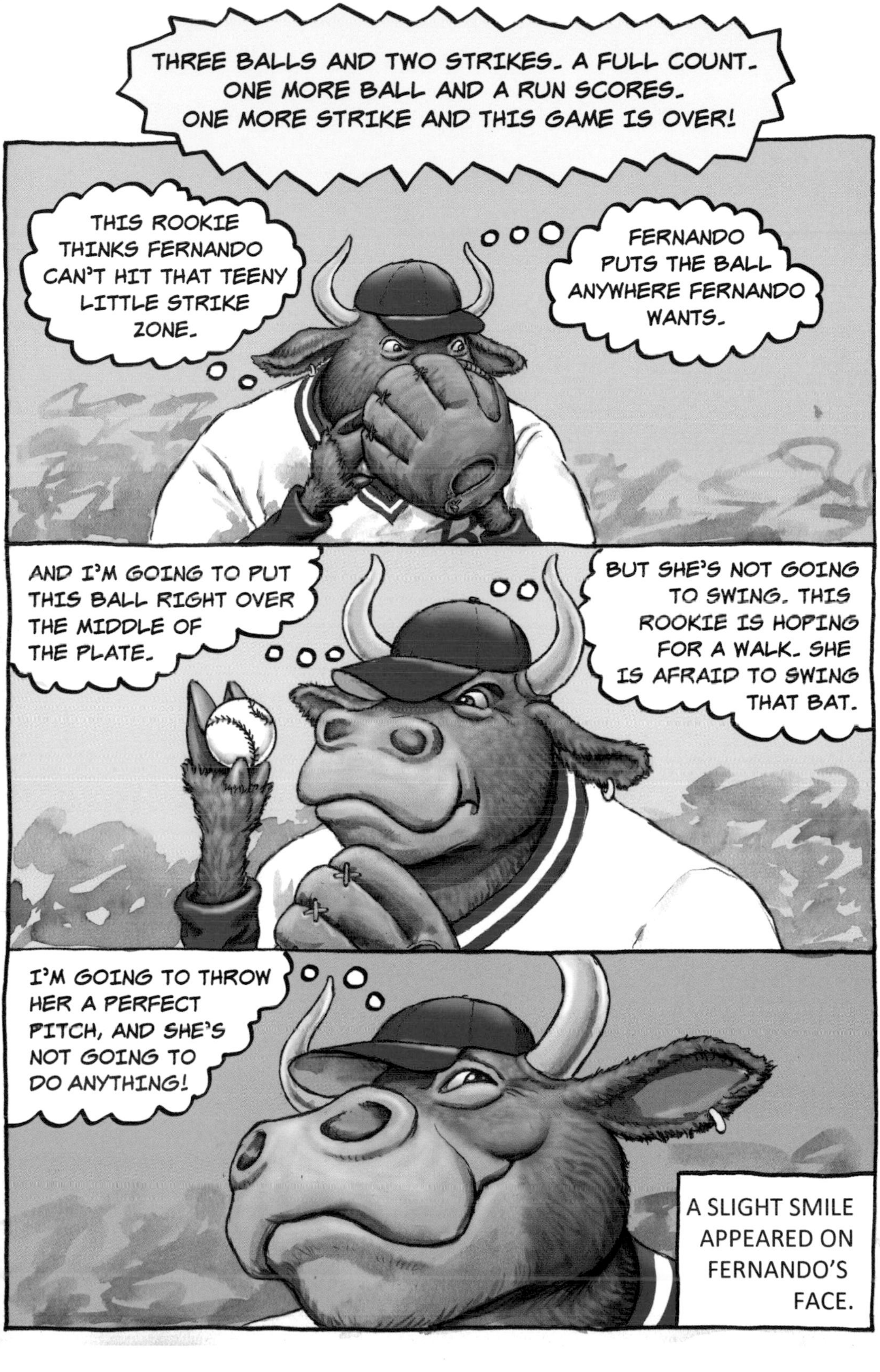
THREE BALLS AND TWO STRIKES. A FULL COUNT. ONE MORE BALL AND A RUN SCORES. ONE MORE STRIKE AND THIS GAME IS OVER!
THIS ROOKIE THINKS FERNANDO CAN'T HIT THAT TEENY LITTLE STRIKE ZONE.
FERNANDO PUTS THE BALL ANYWHERE FERNANDO WANTS.
AND I'M GOING TO PUT THIS BALL RIGHT OVER THE MIDDLE OF THE PLATE.
BUT SHE'S NOT GOING TO SWING. THIS ROOKIE IS HOPING FOR A WALK. SHE IS AFRAID TO SWING THAT BAT.
I'M GOING TO THROW HER A PERFECT PITCH, AND SHE'S NOT GOING TO DO ANYTHING!
A SLIGHT SMILE APPEARED ON FERNANDO'S FACE.

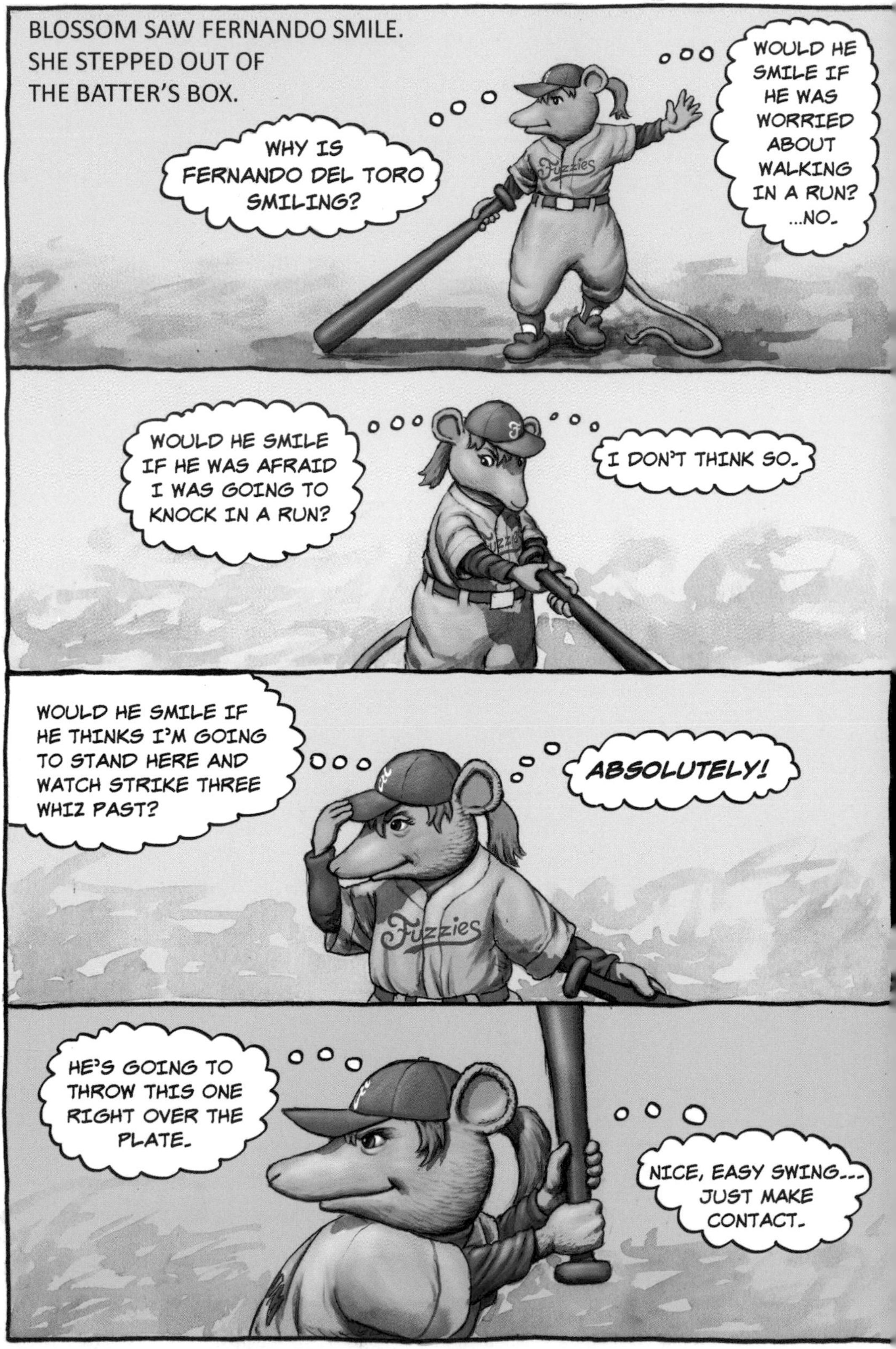
BLOSSOM SAW FERNANDO SMILE. SHE STEPPED OUT OF THE BATTER'S BOX.
WHY IS FERNANDO DEL TORO SMILING?
WOULD HE SMILE IF HE WAS WORRIED ABOUT WALKING IN A RUN? ...NO.
WOULD HE SMILE IF HE WAS AFRAID I WAS GOING TO KNOCK IN A RUN?
I DON'T THINK SO.
WOULD HE SMILE IF HE THINKS I'M GOING TO STAND HERE AND WATCH STRIKE THREE WHIZ PAST?
ABSOLUTELY!
HE'S GOING TO THROW THIS ONE RIGHT OVER THE PLATE.
NICE, EASY SWING... JUST MAKE CONTACT.

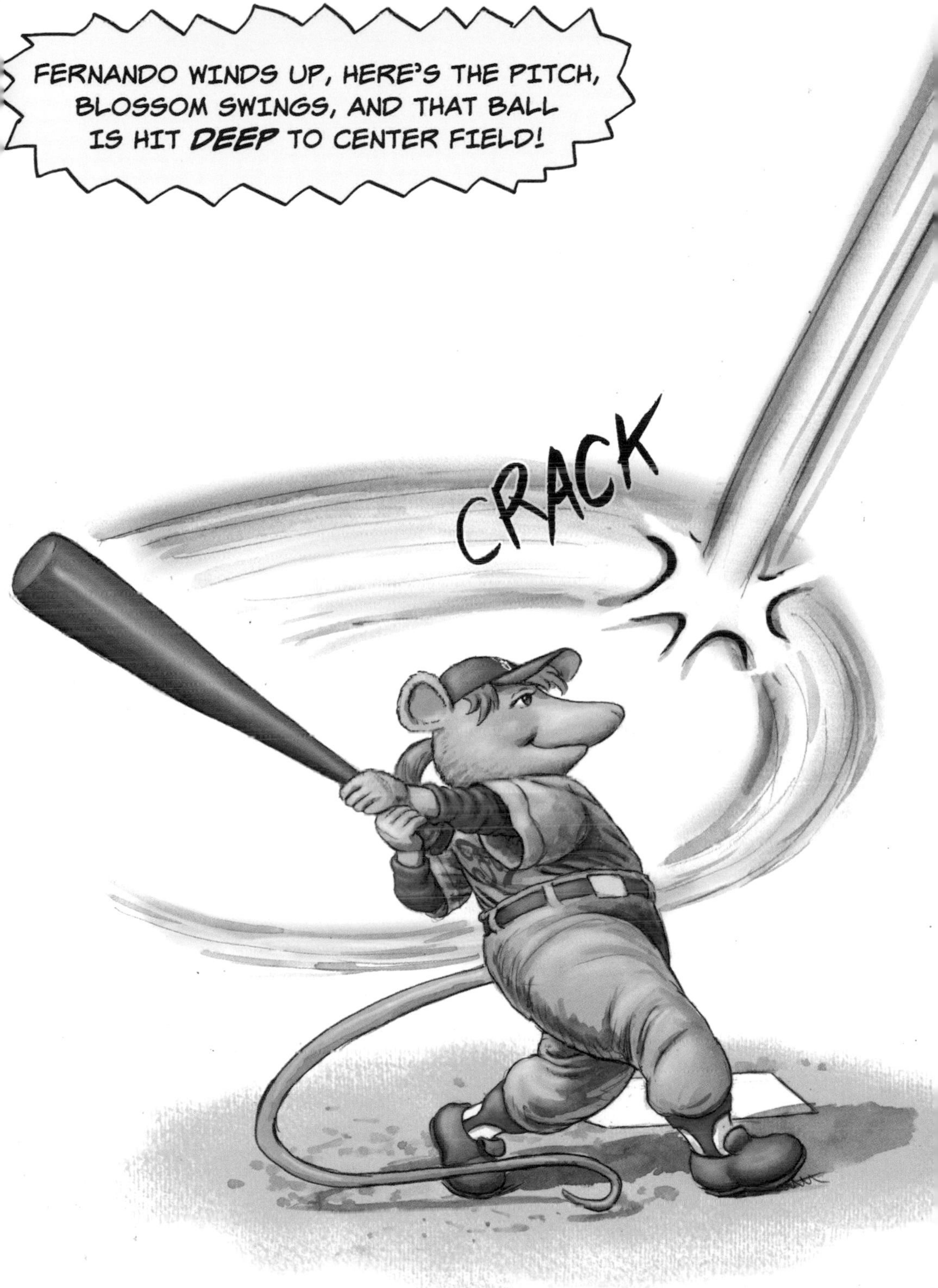
FERNANDO WINDS UP, HERE'S THE PITCH, BLOSSOM SWINGS, AND THAT BALL IS HIT ***DEEP*** TO CENTER FIELD!
CRACK

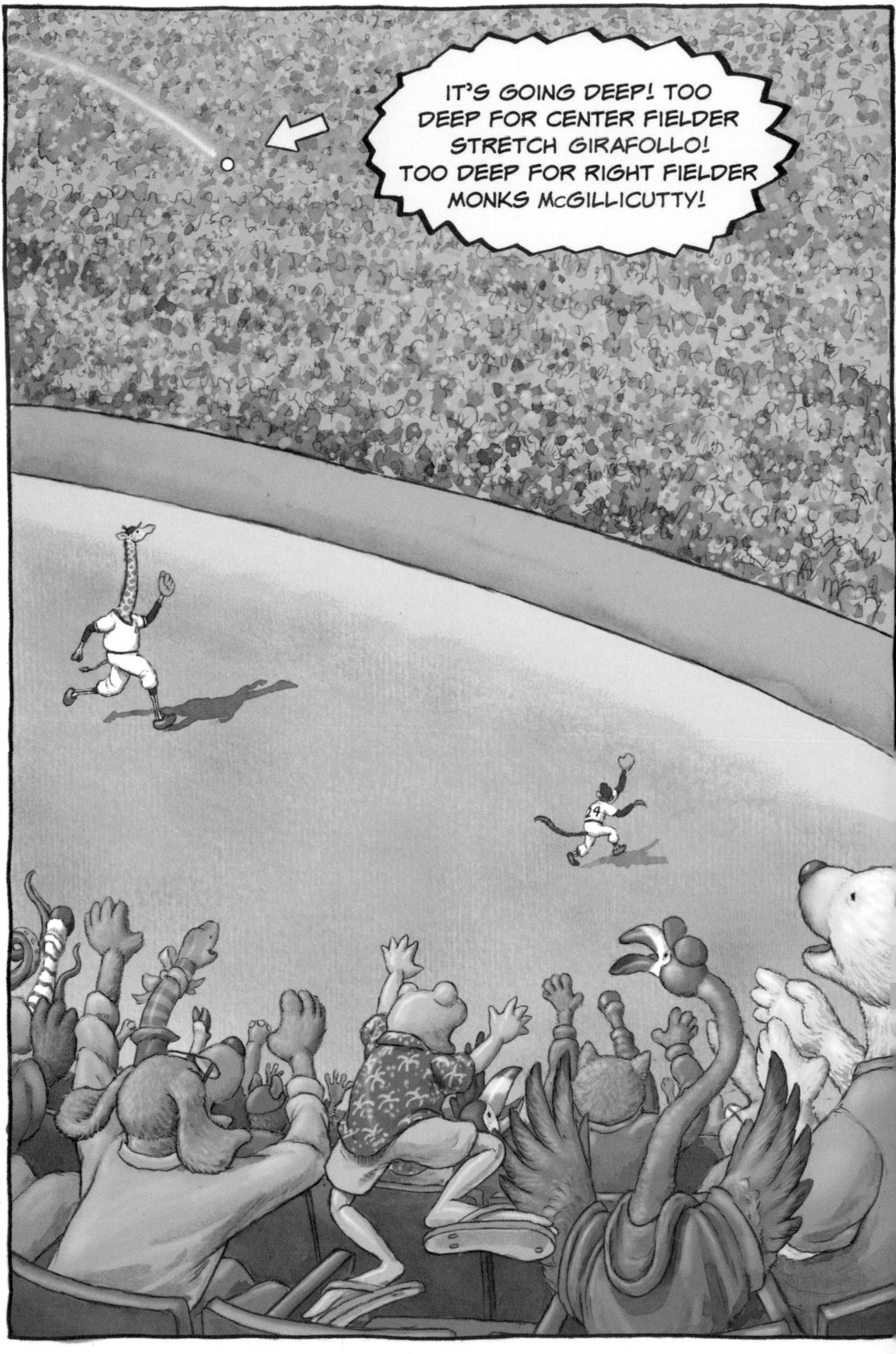
IT'S GOING DEEP! TOO DEEP FOR CENTER FIELDER STRETCH GIRAFOLLO! TOO DEEP FOR RIGHT FIELDER MONKS McGILLICUTTY!

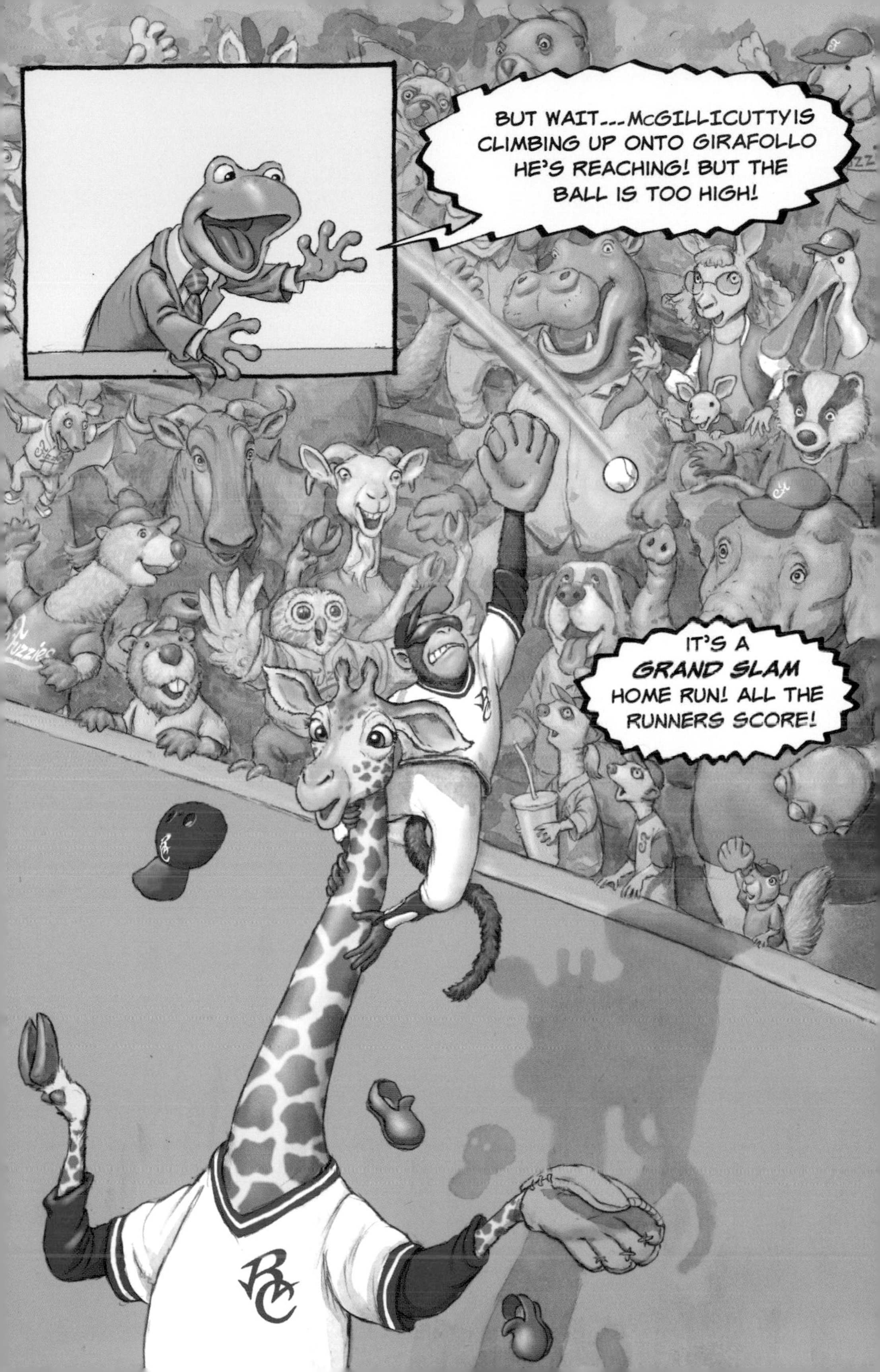
BUT WAIT...McGILLICUTTY IS CLIMBING UP ONTO GIRAFOLLO HE'S REACHING! BUT THE BALL IS TOO HIGH!
IT'S A GRAND SLAM HOME RUN! ALL THE RUNNERS SCORE!

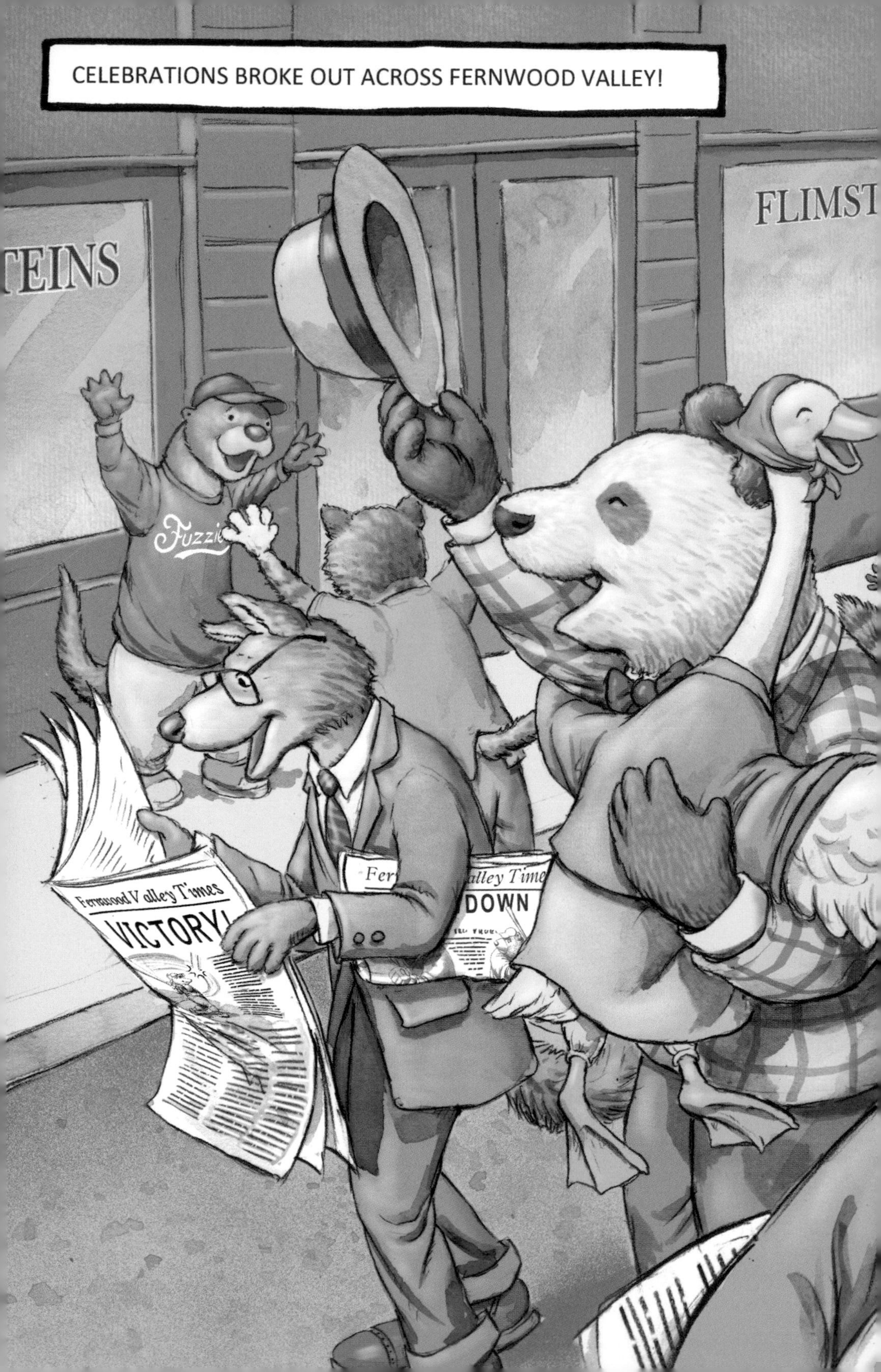
CELEBRATIONS BROKE OUT ACROSS FERNWOOD VALLEY!
TEINS
FLIMST
Fuzzie
Fernwood Valley Times
VICTORY!
DOWN

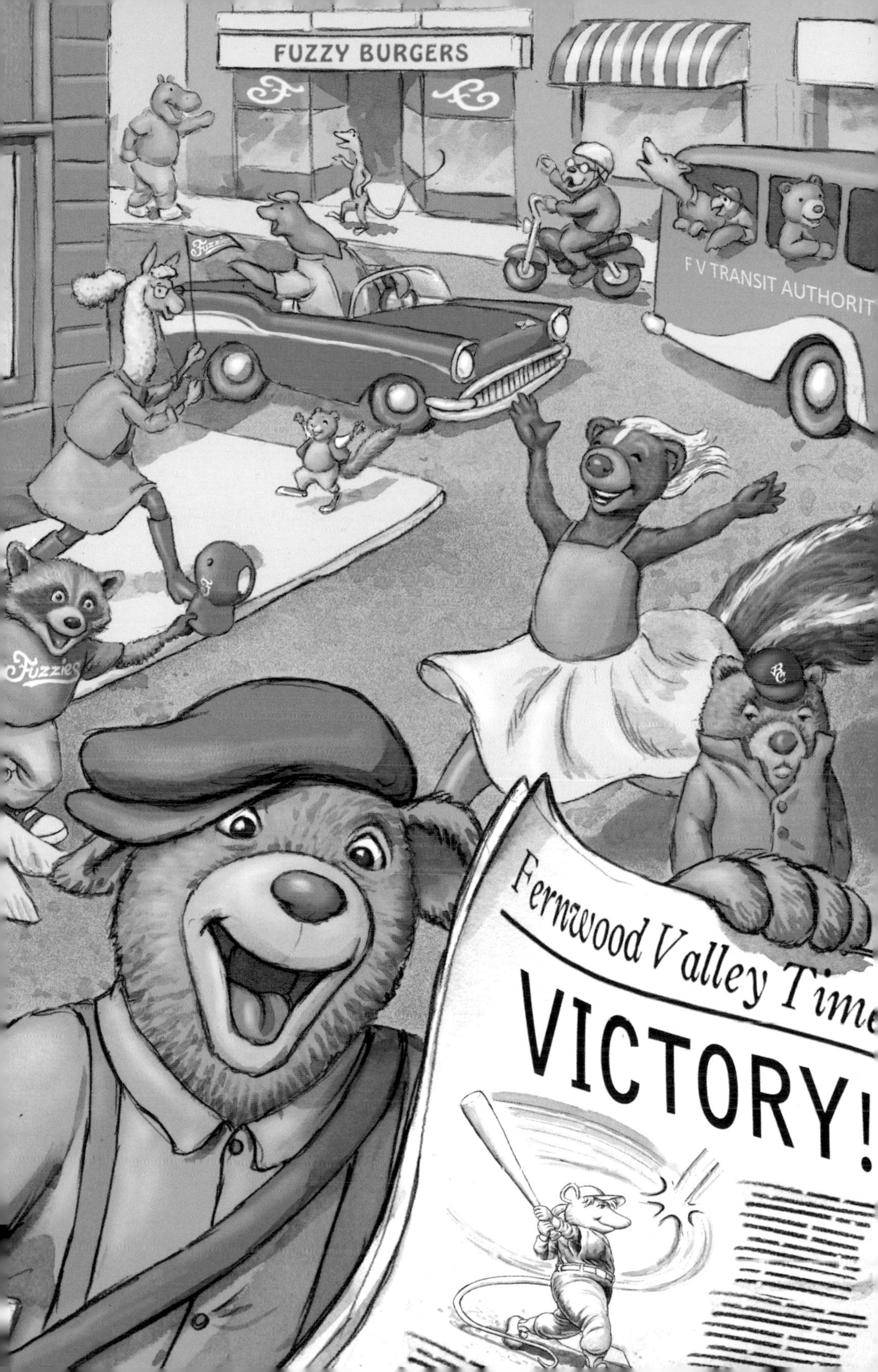
FUZZY BURGERS
Fuzzies
F V TRANSIT AUTHORIT
Fuzzies
Fernwood Valley Time
VICTORY!

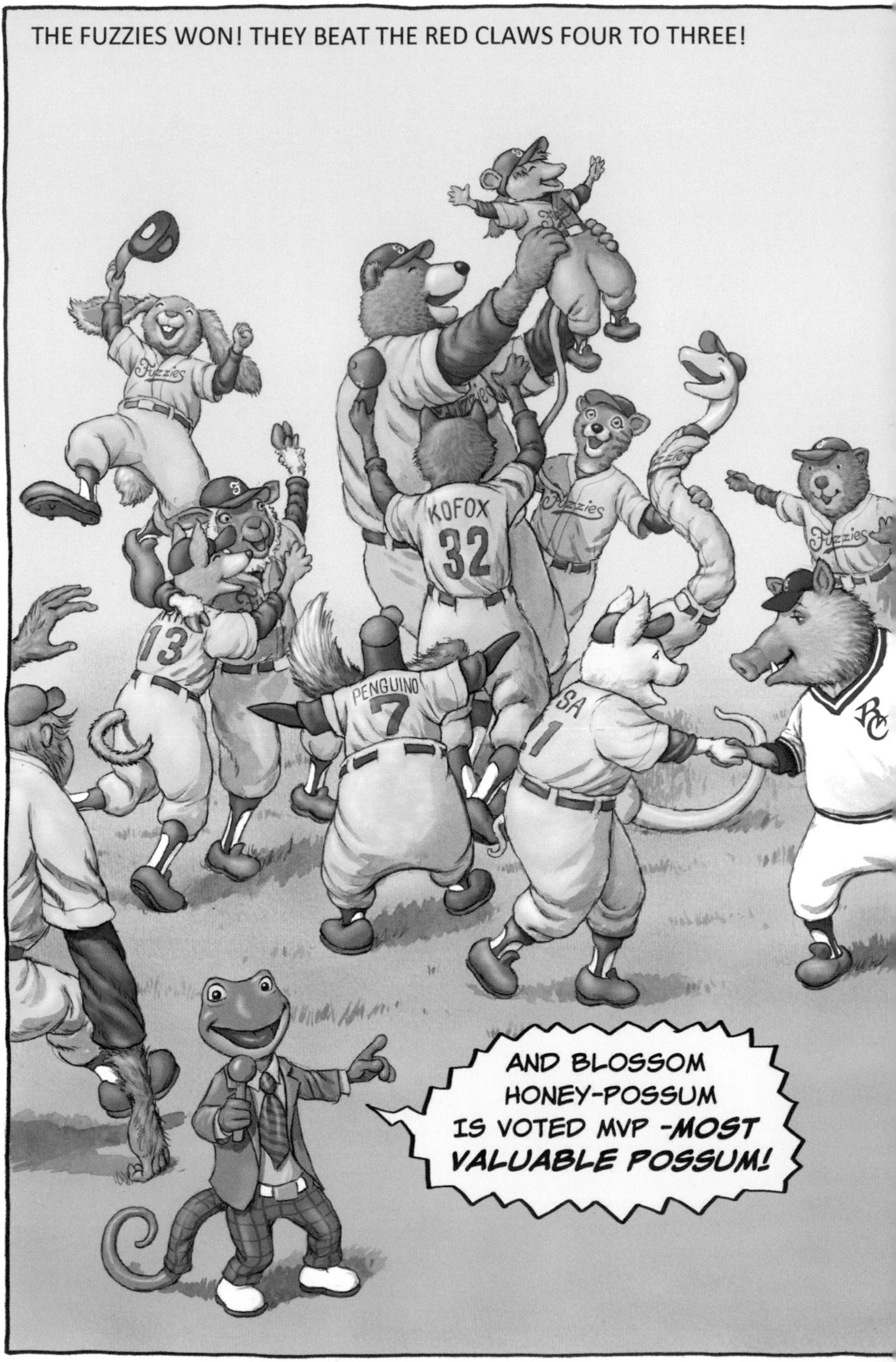
THE FUZZIES WON! THEY BEAT THE RED CLAWS FOUR TO THREE!
Fuzzies
KOFOX
32
13
PENGUINO
7
AND BLOSSOM HONEY-POSSUM IS VOTED MVP -*MOST VALUABLE POSSUM!*

THE END

AND NOW A MESSAGE FROM FERNWOOD VALLEY FUZZIES
ALL-STAR CATCHER HAMMY SOSA.

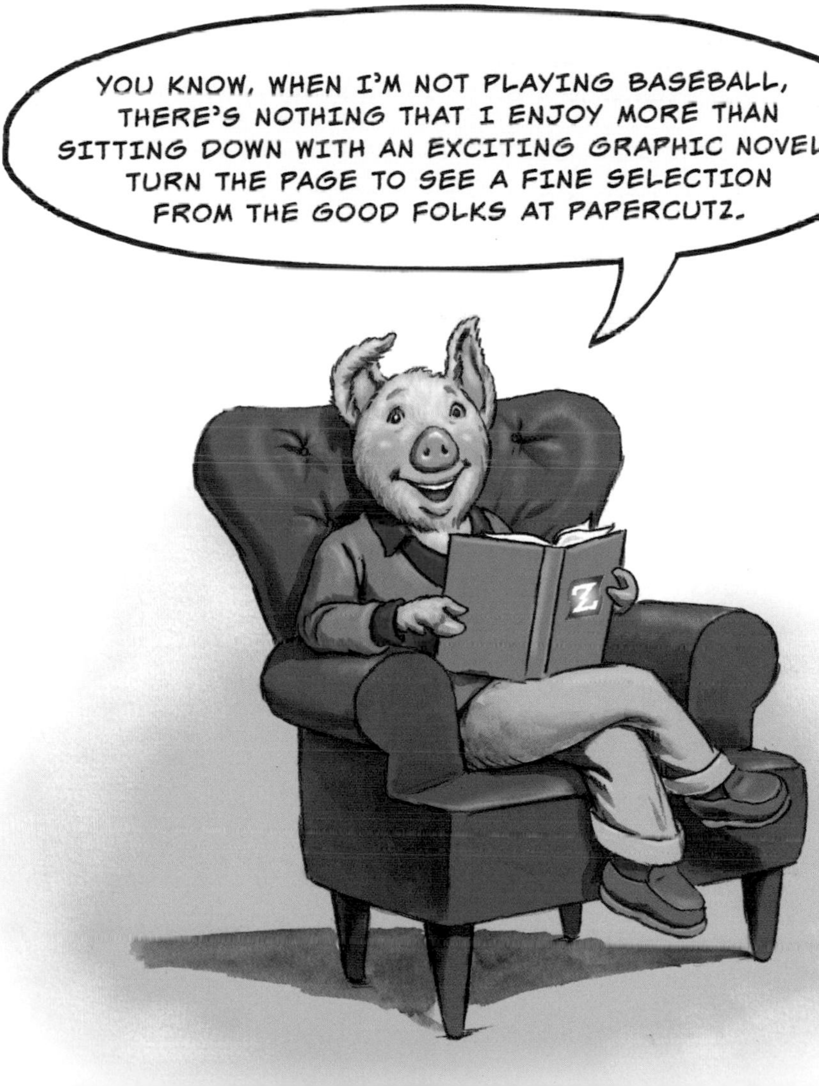
YOU KNOW, WHEN I'M NOT PLAYING BASEBALL, THERE'S NOTHING THAT I ENJOY MORE THAN SITTING DOWN WITH AN EXCITING GRAPHIC NOVEL! TURN THE PAGE TO SEE A FINE SELECTION FROM THE GOOD FOLKS AT PAPERCUTZ.

Special Preview of Fuzzy Baseball #2 "Ninja Baseball Blast"

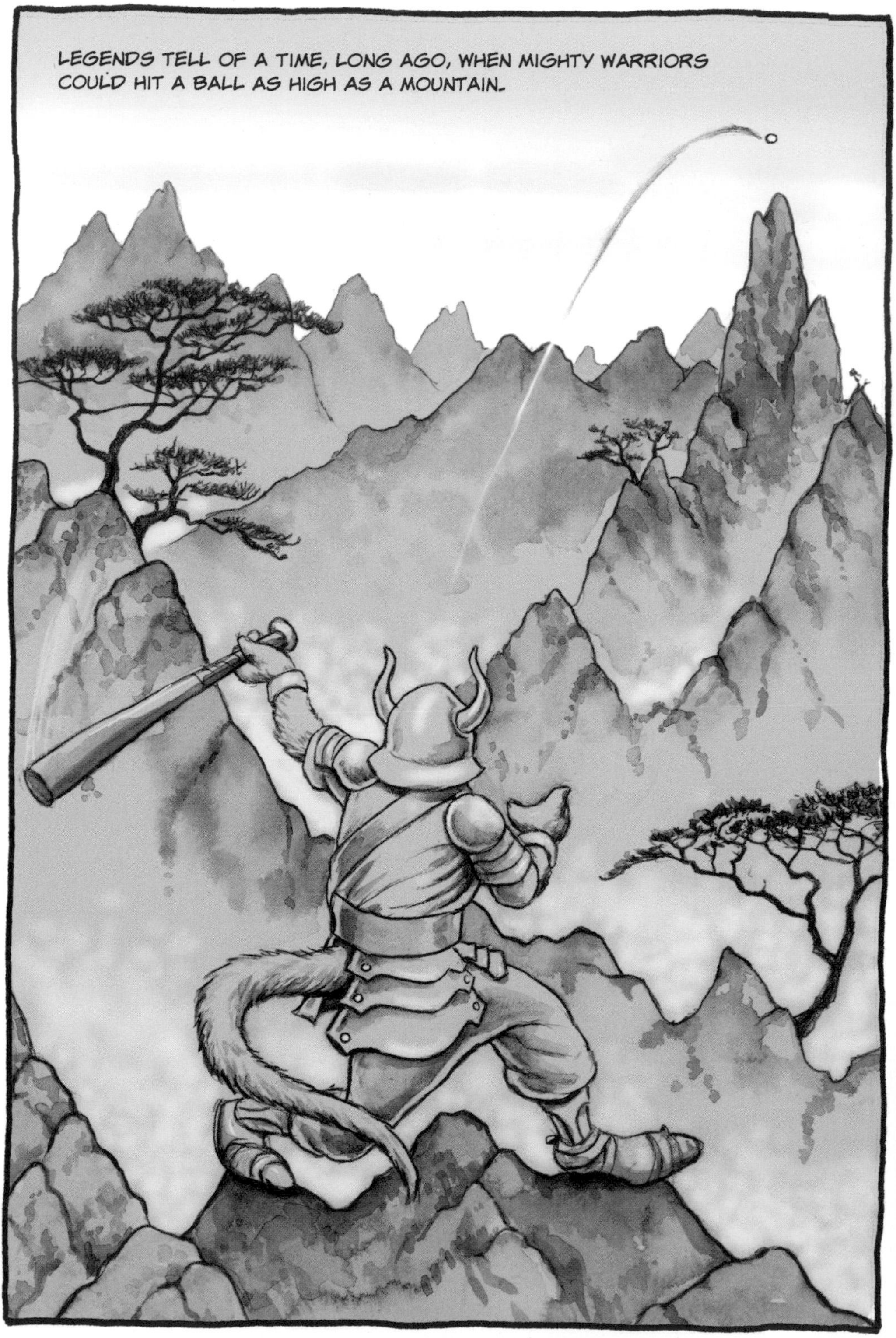
LEGENDS TELL OF A TIME, LONG AGO, WHEN MIGHTY WARRIORS COULD HIT A BALL AS HIGH AS A MOUNTAIN.

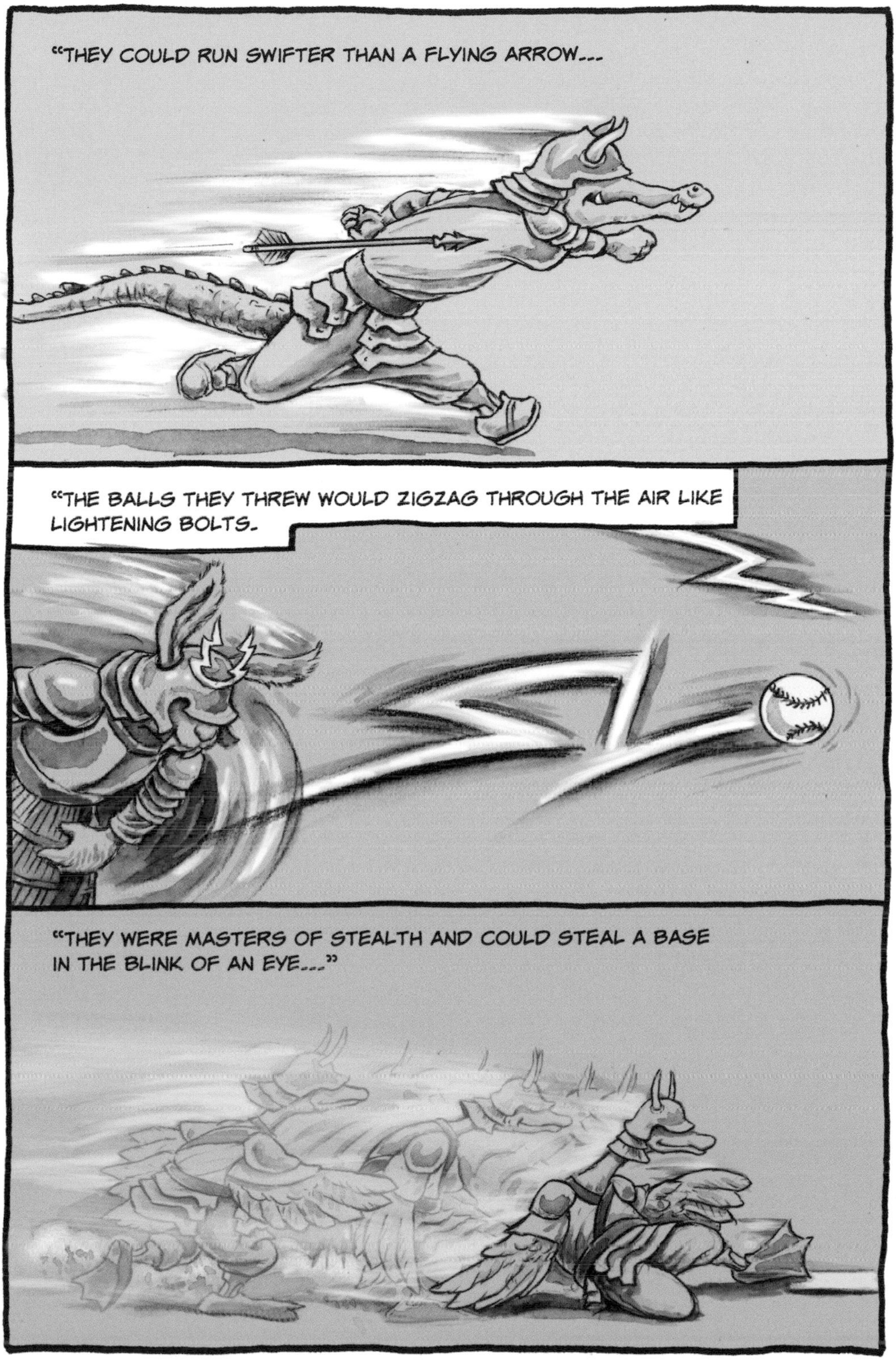
"THEY COULD RUN SWIFTER THAN A FLYING ARROW...
"THE BALLS THEY THREW WOULD ZIGZAG THROUGH THE AIR LIKE LIGHTENING BOLTS.
"THEY WERE MASTERS OF STEALTH AND COULD STEAL A BASE IN THE BLINK OF AN EYE..."

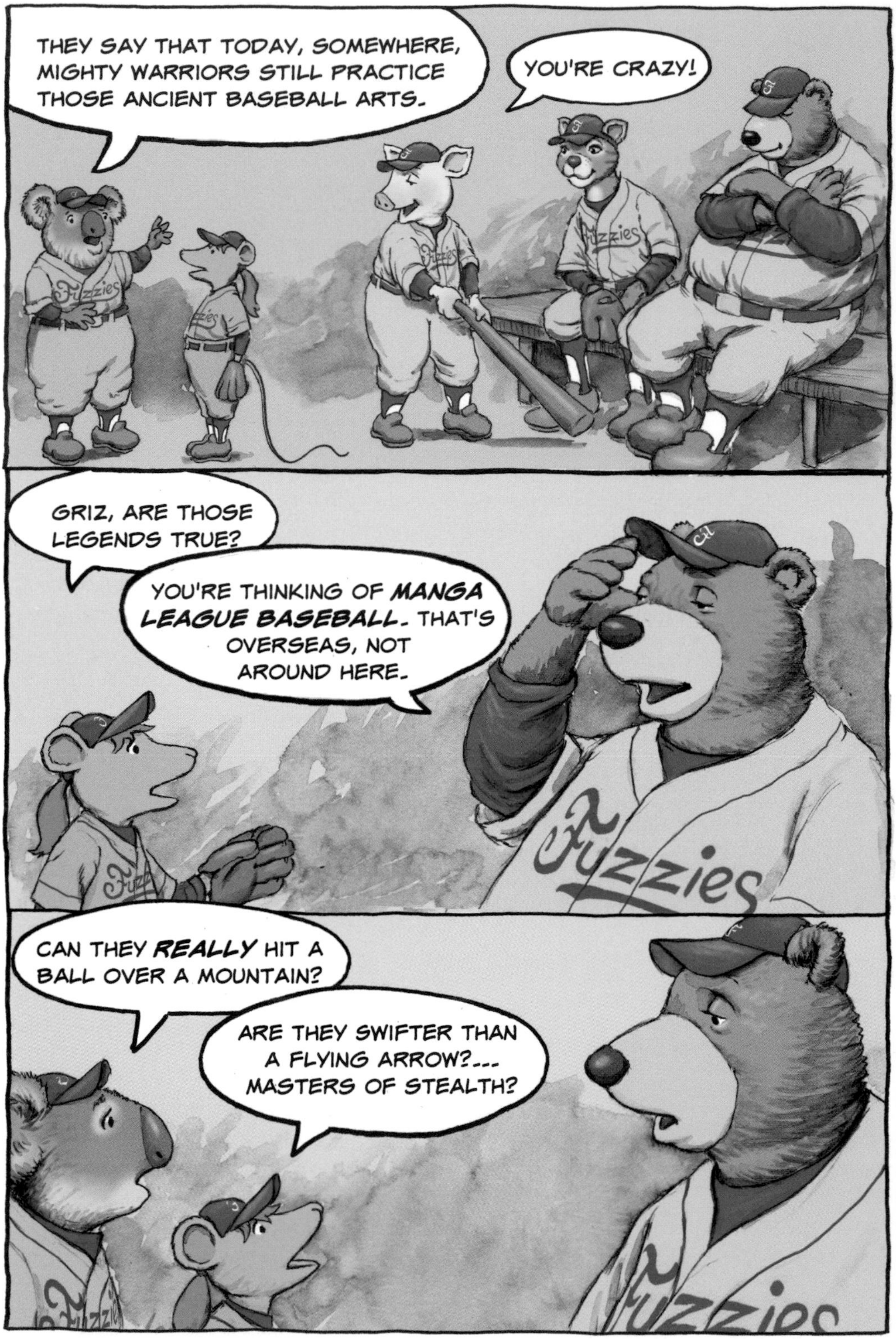
THEY SAY THAT TODAY, SOMEWHERE, MIGHTY WARRIORS STILL PRACTICE THOSE ANCIENT BASEBALL ARTS.
YOU'RE CRAZY!
GRIZ, ARE THOSE LEGENDS TRUE?
YOU'RE THINKING OF MANGA LEAGUE BASEBALL. THAT'S OVERSEAS, NOT AROUND HERE.
CAN THEY REALLY HIT A BALL OVER A MOUNTAIN?
ARE THEY SWIFTER THAN A FLYING ARROW?... MASTERS OF STEALTH?

Don't Miss Fuzzy Baseball #2 "Ninja Baseball Blast"

WATCH OUT FOR PAPERCUTZ

Welcome to the first, fast- (and foul-) ball-filled FUZZY BASEBALL graphic novel, by the home team's John Steven Gurney, from Papercutz, those denizens of the dugout dedicated to publishing great graphic novels for all ages. I'm Jim Salicrup, Editor-in-Chief and Head Coach.

FUZZY BASEBALL combines America's favorite pastime with two other All-American cultural traditions: comicbooks and funny animals. Like most "funny animals," the characters in FUZZY BASEBALL act far more like humans than actual animals. Papercutz publishes a lot of books filled with comics—called "graphic novels"—that feature animals. We start with the very first animals that ever walked the earth, in DINOSAURS, a light-hearted, but fact-filled four volume graphic novel series. But the dino action doesn't stop there! DINOSAUR EXPLORERS sends a group of kids and scientists back in time—even before there were dinosaurs—to trace the origins of these creatures from the Paleozoic to the Cenozoic! And if you want to see a Sci-Fi twist on the future of dinosaurs, check out MANOSAURS—a group of teenage dinosaurs who are half human and half dinosaur.

But we don't only publish graphic novels about extinct creatures. We also publish a lot of graphic novels about cats! So many, that we should probably change our company name from Papercutz to Papercatz! There's PUSSYCAT, a typical housecat and his wacky adventures—written and drawn by Peyo, the world-famous creator of THE SMURFS! CHLOE, the star of her own Charmz series also has a pet cat called Cartoon. He's become so popular that there will soon be the CHLOE'S CAT CARTOON graphic novel. Also coming soon is CAT & CAT, about a girl named Cathy and her cat.

We even published a graphic novel about what seems to be a regular cat, but she actually talks...and is a movie star. You have to get SCARLETT to see what we're talking about.

From cats to mice, let's talk about a certain fa*mouse* reporter... If you like your funny animals to be a bit more human, like the cast of FUZZY BASEBALL, then you'll love GERONIMO STILTON REPORTER! He's a mouse who is always chasing after a big story for *The Rodent's Gazette*, the number one newspaper in New Mouse City. Perhaps you've even seen his animated adventures on Netflix or Amazon Prime? If so, you'll also enjoy the Papercutz GERONIMO STILTON REPORTER graphic novels.

Then there're the great Nickelodeon characters we publish... SANJAY AND CRAIG features one "funny animal"—Craig, the talking snake—in an otherwise human world. HARVEY BEAKS lives in a world of his own in a mysterious wooded area. BREADWINNERS features SwaySway and Buhdeuce, two talking ducks on the planet Pondgea who deliver bread in their rocket van. PIG GOAT BANANA CRICKET takes place on a world where everything seems to be alive—even bananas! Of course, our biggest hit Nickelodeon title is THE LOUD HOUSE, based on the adventures of Lincoln Loud and his ten sisters—but they have quite a few pets as well: Fangs, a bat; Walt, a bird; Bitey, a mouse; Hops, a frog; Geo, a hamster; Cliff, a cat; and Charles, a dog.

Believe it or not, Papercutz publishes plenty of graphic novels that feature humans, but even as I say that, I notice that the latest THE ONLY LIVING GIRL graphic novel features a story with all sorts of creatures and monsters! I'm not sure if Papercutz is a comics publishing company or a zoo! Hey, what does it matter if they're all great comics?

And speaking of great comics, don't miss another all-new FUZZY BASEBALL story in which the Fernwood Valley Fuzzies travel to Japan to face the Sashimi City Ninjas! Don't miss FUZZY BASEBALL BLAST, available at booksellers everywhere. Check out the next few pages for a special sneak preview!

Thanks,

Jim

STAY IN TOUCH!

EMAIL:	salicrup@papercutz.com
WEB:	papercutz.com
TWITTER:	@papercutzgn
INSTAGRAM:	@papercutzgn
FACEBOOK:	PAPERCUTZGRAPHICNOVELS
REGULAR MAIL:	Papercutz, 160 Broadway, Suite 700, East Wing, New York, NY 10038

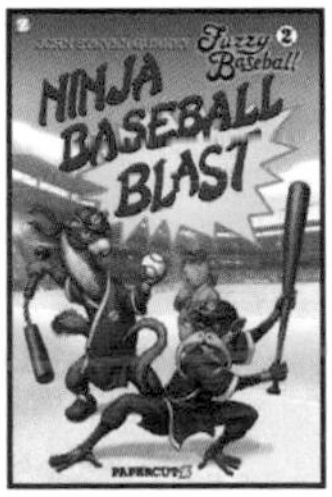

Fuzzy Baseball! 2
NINJA BASEBALL BLAST

A MEMO FROM
THE COMMISSIONER

FERNWOOD VALLEY FUZZIES

JOHN STEVEN GURNEY
COMMISSIONER

John Steven Gurney grew up outside of Philadelphia, Pennsylvania watching helplessly as the Philadelphia Phillies continually lost to the Cincinnati Reds, (and pretty much every other team as well). Then, miraculously, the Phillies won the 1980 World Series, and it seemed as if miracles were possible. John studied Illustration at Pratt Institute in Brooklyn, New York, and was a New York Mets fan in 1986 when the Mets won the World Series. And John was a Boston Red Sox fan in 2004, raising his family in Vermont, when the Red Sox broke free of their 86 year old curse and won the World Series.

As a child John never played organized baseball, only pick-up games in his neighborhood. As an adult he coached tee-ball, was an assistant coach for Small Fry, and was a helpful parent during Little League.

Fuzzy Baseball is John's first graphic novel. John is the author and illustrator of the picture book **Dinosaur Train**, and he is the illustrator of over 140 chapter books, including The **A to Z Mysteries** and **The Bailey School Kids**.

LEARN MORE ABOUT JOHN AT JOHNSTEVENGURNEY.COM.